Coyote and the Thunderbird

Praise For *Coyote and the Thunderbird*

"James Lenfestey has found a character that a lot of us see in ourselves. This is contemporary mythology at its best."

—Eric Utne, founder, *The Utne Reader*

"James Lenfestey teases the very best humor and contradictions of the elusive trickster in his stories. The trickster is the comic healer in literature, and we are teased to tears and healed with humor in *Coyote and the Thunderbird: New Tales for the Book of Coyote*."

—Gerald Vizenor, author of *Theatre of Chance: Native Celebrities of Nothing*

"Coyote has always been delightful to me and I think Jim handles his stories well. I think the spell of Coyote is open to anyone brave enough to appreciate him."

—Diane Glancy, award-winning Native American poet, author, playwright, and retired professor of Native American Literature at Macalester College

"A joy to read! Up to his old tricks again, Coyote stirs the pot, hilarious and wild and wise. Read these new adventures and be ready when he shows up at your door!"

—James Thornton, Founder of ClientEarth and author of *The Feynman Challenge*

"With his witty and vigorous narrative style, Jim Lenfestey skillfully plays with the timeless trickster archetype."

—Paul Winter, Grammy-winning founder of The Paul Winter Consort

Coyote and the Thunderbird

New Tales for the Book of Coyote

James P. Lenfestey

Foreword by Lewis Hyde, author of
Trickster Makes This World and *The Gift*

Minneapolis

FIRST EDITION 2026

Coyote and the Thunderbiord: New Tales for the Book of Coyote

10 9 8 7 6 5 4 3 2 1

ISBN: 978-1-962834-71-1

Cover image, "Shuffle Off to Buffalo," used by permission of the Minnesota Museum of American Art.

Author photograph on back cover by John Walsh (hearthtonemn.com)

Cover and interior design by Gary Lindberg

Also by James P. Lenfestey

Time Remaining. Body Odes, Praise Songs, Oddities, Amazements, 2024

Stephen Crane: Selected Poems, editor, 2022

Seasons of the Urban Coyote: Essays on Family, Community, and the Search for Peace and Justice, 2021

The Uncommon Speech of Paradise: Poems on the Art of Poetry, co-editor, 2021

Thirteen September Moons: A Love Story, 2020

East Bluff: Mackinac Poems Old & New, 2019

A Marriage Book: 50 Years of Poems from a Marriage, 2017

If Bees Are Few: A Hive of Bee Poems, editor, 2016

Seeking the Cave: A Pilgrimage to Cold Mountain, 2016

Earth in Anger: Twenty-Five Poems of Love and Despair for Planet Earth, 2013

Robert Bly in This World, co-editor, 2011

Low Down and Coming On: A Feast of Delicious and Dangerous Poems about Pigs, editor, 2010

A Cartload of Scrolls: 100 Poems in the Manner of Tang Dynasty Poet Han-Shan, 2007

Into the Goodhue County Jail: Poems to Free Prisoners, 2008

The Toothed and Clever World, 2006

Han-shan is the Cure for Warts, 2005

Affection for Spiders, 2005

Saying Grace: Wisconsin Poems, 2004

Odalisque, 2004

The Urban Coyote: Howlings on Family, Community, and the Search for Peace and Quiet, 2000

Table of Contents

"In picaresque tales, in carnivals and revels, in magic rites of healing, in man's religious fears and exaltations, this phantom of the trickster haunts the mythology of all ages, sometimes in quite unmistakable form, sometimes in strangely modulated guise."

—"On the Psychology of the Trickster figure," Carl Jung

"Yet the always traveling, always lustful, breaker-of-limits side of the Trickster could destroy any human poet who got locked into it. The Trickster is a delightful literary conceit, but an unpredictable Ally, dangerous and very potent."

—"The Incredible Survival of Coyote," Gary Snyder

"The trickster secures his earth, his urban places now, and then he dreams out of familiar time and space."

—*Earthdivers*, Gerald Vizenor

“Trickster stayed at that village for a long time and raised many children. One day he said, ‘Well, this is about as long as I will stay here. I have been here a long time. Now I am going to go around the earth again and visit different people for my children are all grown up. I was not created for what I am doing here.’”

from the Winnebago (Ho-Chunk) Trickster Cycle, Paul Radin

“Everything in the world, said my father, is big with jest and has wit in it, and instruction too if we can but find it out.”

—Lawrence Sterne, *Tristram Shandy*

“Foolery, sir, doth walk around the orb like the sun, it shines everywhere!”

—Feste, *Twelfth Night*, William Shakespeare

For Trickster tales and tellers and listeners around the world.

Foreword

From *Trickster Makes This World: Mischief, Myth, and Art*

by Lewis Hyde

If this myth contains a story about incrementally increasing intelligence, where does it lead? What happens after the carnivore gets up to ten?

There is a great deal of folklore about coyotes in the American West. One story has it that in the old days sheep farmers tried to get rid of wolves and coyotes by putting out animal carcasses laced with strychnine. The wolves, they say, were killed in great numbers, but the coyotes wised up and avoided these traps. Another story has it that when trappers set metal leg traps they will catch muskrat and mink and fox and skunk, but coyote only rarely. Coyotes develop their own relationship to the trap; as one naturalist has written, "It is difficult to escape the conclusion that coyotes ... have a sense of humor. How else to explain, for instance, the well-known propensity of experienced coyotes to dig up traps, turn them over, and urinate or defecate on them?"

With this image we move into a third relationship between tricksters and traps. When a coyote defecates on a trap he is neither predator nor prey but some third thing. A fragment of a native Tlingit story from Alaska will help us name that thing:

> [Raven] came to a place where many people were encamped fishing... He entered a house and asked what they used for bait. They said, "Fat." Then he said, "Let me see you put enough on your hooks for bait," and he noticed carefully how they baited and handled their hooks. The next time they went out, he walked off behind a point and went underwater to get this bait. Now they got bites and pulled up quickly, but there was nothing on their hooks.

Raven eventually gets in trouble for this little trick (the fishermen steal his beak and he has to pull an elaborate return-ruse to get it back), but for now the point is simply that in the relationship between fish and fishermen this trickster stands to the side and takes on a third role.

A similar motif appears in Africa with the Zulu trickster known as Thlokunyana. Thlokunyana is imagined to be a small man, "the size of a weasel," and in fact one of his other names also refers to a red weasel with a black-tipped tail. A Zulu storyteller describes this animal as cleverer than all others, for its cunning is great. If a trap is set for a wild cat, the weasel comes immediately to the trap and takes away the mouse which is placed there for the cat. It takes it out first; and when the cat comes the mouse has been already eaten by the weasel.

If a hunter does manage to trap this tricky weasel, he will have bad luck. A kind of jinx or magical influence remains in the trap that has caught a weasel and that influence forever after "stands in the way" of the trap's power; it will no longer catch game.

Coyote in fact and folklore, Raven and Thlokunyana in mythology—in each of these cases, trickster gets wise to the bait and is therefore all the harder to catch. The coyote who avoids a strychnined carcass is perhaps the simplest case; he does not get poisoned but he also gets nothing to eat. Raven and Thlokunyana are more cunning in this regard; they are bait-thief tricksters who separate the trap from the meat and eat the meat. Each of these tales has a predator-prey relationship in it—the fish and the fishermen, for example—but the bait thief doesn't enter directly into that oppositional eating game. A parasite or epizoon, he feeds his belly while standing just outside the conflict between hunter and hunted. From that position the bait thief becomes a kind of critic of the usual rules of the eating game and as such subverts them, so that the traps he visits lose their influence. What trapper's pride could remain unshaken once he's read Coyote's commentary?

In all these stories, trickster must do more than feed his belly; he must do so without himself getting eaten. Trickster's intelligence springs from appetite in two ways; it simultaneously seeks to satiate hunger and to subvert all hunger not its own. This last is an important theme. In the Okanagan creation story, the Great Spirit, having told Coyote that he must show the New People how to catch salmon, goes on to say: "I have important work for you to do ... There are many bad creatures on earth. You will have to kill them, otherwise they will eat the New People. When you do this, the New People will honor you ... They will honor you for killing the People-devouring monsters and for teaching ... all the ways of living." In North America, trickster stepped in to defeat the monsters who used to feed on humans.

The myth says, then, that there are large, devouring forces in this world, and that trickster's intelligence arose not just to feed himself but to outwit these other eaters. Typically, this meeting is oppositional—the prey outwitting the predator. The bait thief suggests a different, nonoppositional strategy. Here trickster feeds himself where predator and prey meet, but rather than entering the game on their terms he plays with its rules. Perhaps, then, another force behind trickster's cunning is the desire to remove himself from the eating game altogether, or at least see how far out he can get and still feed his belly (for if he were to stop eating entirely he would no longer be trickster).

—Lewis Hyde, 1998
(used by permission of the author)

Preface

The first book of Coyote is the ongoing oral tradition of the Indigenous American people and their various Trickster characters. It is large, funny, complex and growing. The second book is *Giving Birth to Thunder, Sleeping with His Daughter: Coyote Builds North America,* a compilation of traditional Indigenous American trickster stories by Barry Holstun Lopez (1970) that was the first, to my knowledge, to attach the name Coyote to many of the diverse trickster heroes from throughout North America. There are many other fine Trickster story collections. A third book of Coyote would include modern fictional adaptations, such as those of Anishinabe writer Gerald Vizenor. A fourth book, if I may call it that, are the antic Coyote images made by the Miwok artist Harry Fonseca, four of which hung on my office brick walls in downtown Minneapolis and which came to life in these stories: Coyote as Uncle Sam, Coyote singing with the Res Girls, Coyote dancing "Shuffle Off to Buffalo," and Coyote as a formidable woman. These images are now at the Minnesota Museum of American Art in St Paul and can be seen online and in many museums and galleries.

After hanging out with Trickster stories for more than twenty years while teaching Native American literature and the Literature of Comedy (in which they were featured) and later as a marketing communications specialist surrounded by Harry Fonseca Coyote images on my office walls, I found them getting under my skin. Finally, my own Trickster stories began to pounce out of me. While driving. While sleeping. And finally, while strolling near the keyboard of my Macintosh. One after another, they pounced onto the screen. Over the years, they wove themselves together into *Coyote and the Thunderbird.* Although Trickster is indeed a "dangerous and unpredictable ally," I take full responsibility for all characters, content, and manner of presentation.

Several of these tales have been published, in slightly different form, in the following publications: "The Origin of Fall," *Loonfeather*; "Coyote Plays Ball," *Minnesota Review of Baseball;* "Coyote Walks the Kid," *Kingfisher;* "Coyote Moves to the City" (published as "Coyote Drives to Work"), *Kingfisher*; "Coyote Camps Out" (published as "Coyote Wears a Hair Shirt"*), Colorado North Review*; and "Coyote Saves White Buffalo Woman," *St. Paul American Indian Center magazine.* Finally, the ball cap worn by Coyote in

"Coyote Plays Ball" is a copy of the actual cap worn by real life Anishinaabe trickster, humorist, writer, and activist Jim Northrup.

*Pronunciation guide. For the purposes of these tales, I hear the three-syllable pronunciation, *kai-o-tee*, and not the two syllable, *kai-oat*, although both are correct in American English. The two-syllable pronunciation is closer to the original Nahuatl, while the three-syllable is closer to the Spanish adaptation. Whatever, these stories work better for my ear if the three-syllable form is heard.

Chapter 1
Coyote and the Thunderbird

Coyote was going along. Prancing through California's golden coastal grass he was, cursing the dry grass poking at his eyes. He pounced over a tall tuft toward a patch of green. Right into some poison oak. "Aieee!" Coyote howled, "this is the pits."

He stood up and gazed out over the Pacific surf rolling in below him carrying mesmerizing messages direct from Polynesia, one sensual message after another. He imagined himself on a Bora Bora beach attended by Gauguin maidens tasting of breadfruit, fragrant with gardenias, all with Ph.Ds from the University of Love. He wanted to be their student.

He inhaled the sea salt air. What's that? An exceptionally funky scent bristled his fur.

Below him, on the shoulder of US Highway 1, the Pacific Coast Highway that scratches the western thigh of North

America, idled the most powerful mythical beast ever dreamed up on the continent, the sleek and elusive Thunderbird. It flamed red in the sun. It huffed choking streams of black bad breath. And it was looking the other way.

"Ahhhhh," exhaled Coyote, his instincts inflamed by the legendary power of such a beast. He had to take it on.

He slinked down the steep bluff and poked his nose through the dry bunch grass at the edge of the road. He shot his eyeballs up, then down the highway (note: even Coyote checks both ways before crossing). All clear. He crouched out, the hot asphalt highway searing his tender footpads, ouch, ouch, keeping low, *ouch ouch*, doing a funky inadvertent Caribbean-style dance step, *ouch ouch ouch*, right up to the rear of the rumbling Thunderbird. His flaming footpads cooling on gravel shoulder, he warily stood up. He glanced inside.

Nobody home. And the keys were in it.

A half-killed twelve pack lay on the passenger seat among a litter of empties. On the floor was a rumpled late edition of the *Weekly World News* with the headline: ALIEN TO MARRY BIGFOOT! Coyote could not resist. He reached in. He had to read that story.

As he leaned over the side of the car, a loud moan erupted behind him. Coyote spun around, teeth bared, fur bristling. The sound again—this time a long *ahhhhhhhhh* coming from behind a nearby boulder, accompanied by the *shissshhhh* of a high-pressure stream. The stream flowed on and on, tumbling toward the ocean below, scouring its own canyon. "Beer," thought Coyote. "From that especially odious mammalian, genus *Homo*, species *sapiens*, subspecies *beergut.*" Coyote reached into his kit bag and fingered his membership card in MADD, Mammals Against Drunk Driving. "*Sapiens*," he mumbled to himself. "What a joke. Thanks to these guys, half my friends are roadkill."

Coyote looked back at the Thunderbird and whistled to himself. What a magnificent creature, he thought while running his paws along the soft contours of the two-seater 1956 convertible, bright red, rust creeping up the wheel wells, salt spray pitting the chrome, black Naugahyde interior roasting in the sun. "Ahhhh," the beast behind the boulder groaned again, and Coyote heard metal teeth grinding together.

Coyote leaped over the side of the Thunderbird, slid onto the black Naugahyde upholstery hot as fresh volcanic ash, *aieee*, whipped his tail under his butt, *whew*, jammed his toes below the dash blinking with lights indicating rapidly overheating cylinders, felt for the clutch and the gas, cranked the gearshift into first, popped the clutch and roared out, spewing shoulder gravel past the open mouth of the emerging big-bellied *Homo sapiens beergut* and far out over the Pacific to scratch the backs of migrating whales.

Coyote leaned back, wind in his whiskers, nose in the air, and howled into the enflamed sky. "I've captured the Thunderbird!" Coyote crowed.

The magnificent red convertible ripped up the coastal highway with its 350 cubic-inch V-8, four on the floor, fast and powerful and quick and old, raucous pitted mufflers, blowing smoke out the back like a coal train, laying down an oil slick like a beached tanker, grabbing corners high over the Pacific like a shoplifter. On the move. "Oooo, I like this," said Coyote, and he began to dream.

He dreamed he was in the Black Hills, in the heart of North America. He dreamed that a crowd of unidentified small mammals dressed in Ragstock clothes and tattered berets was following him around with hammers, chisels and Polaroids. They were taking his picture from every angle as he strolled, stopped, pounced, ate, napped, and howled into the moonlit night. He did some tricks for them, why not? A little eye juggling. Some shapeshifting—from a coyote to a turtle to a buffalo and back again. His forepaws traded insults with one another. The audience went wild at everything he did. Laughter flared. Flashbulbs popped. He was on a roll.

Suddenly the critters gathered around each other in a tight circle, murmuring with excitement as they looked over hundreds of prints spread out on the dirt. "Hey, let me see," said Coyote, leaning into the crowd, curiosity burning. "That one!" they shouted, pointing at one of the Polaroids, erupting in loud cheers. "Hey," said Coyote, "I'm not sure that's the best. . . ." They ignored him, breaking into a dead run for the tallest peak in the Hills, a gray granite spire that emerged from dark-green pines and Badlands dust below. The crowd of creatures surrounded the base of the peak. There were so many of them they completely encircled it. They began chiseling. Stone chips flew everywhere, forming a dangerously slippery talus slope below. Coyote couldn't climb up to watch them. "Who are you?" he howled up into the blistering rain of granite flakes. "We've got a grant," excited voices tumbled back around him. "What's that?" Coyote howled, "Ulysses S. Grant?" "No, no," chiseled the busy reply, "State Arts Board Grant."

"Artists…" Coyote whistled. "I should have known." He turned and trotted down toward the lights of the nearest town, practicing white man disguises along the way while sniffing the breeze for fresh marmot or fresh tourist backpack. He felt the exhilaration that only an intimation of immortality can bring. But when he turned to look back at the granite spire, the peak was buried in the skirts of scudding clouds. "I should have known," Coyote said. He trotted on down toward town.

He passed a hitchhiker like a blurred archangel. She reclined on a roadside boulder, a furry odalisque, her soft quizzical form etched against the horizon of Pacific sunset, cool beneath the twisted shadow of an ancient Monterey pine. Below her a freshwater stream dipped through a slash of ferns to lose its sweet water virginity in the ocean pulsing below, 35,000 parts per million sodium chloride. Her incandescent pheromones radiated into the ozone sunset and into the deepest neural receptors of Coyote's reptile brain.

He hit the brakes like a rock from an avalanche. He backed up like a teenager in a high school parking lot.

"Jump in, Coyote Woman," grinned Coyote, leaning over to open the passenger door. "I'll take you wherever you are going."

She slowly stretched herself, betraying relaxed confidence, as if she knew all along he was coming. Coyote watched her tongue lick the fiery sunset. Her shining yellow eyes looked right through him to his viscous, molten core. She casually ambled across the highway and carefully inspected the passenger seat. She leaned in and stuffed the *Weekly World News* and beer cans under the seat. "We can read and recycle later," she grinned. Then she slid her tail under her and pulled the door closed, wafting an ancient perfume so pungent it made Coyote's ears flop down and toenails tremble.

As Thunderbird pulled back onto the highway with a snappy spray of gravel, she lay back with her wet nose poised in the air. Before he hit second gear, she had rolled over and grabbed his gas pedal thigh with both her paws. "Tell me a story," she whispered, her cool nose burrowed into his flying ear, her own ears laid back, her eyelids weighted, her smile wide and deep as the Japanese current. "I hear you're good at that. Tell me a story. And then I'll tell you about all the children we're going to have."

"Children?" said Coyote, the front wheels of the Thunderbird clicking the guard rail posts, the ribbon of coast highway unfurling in front of him. "Children? What are those? Where do they come from?"

A few miles further up the coast, Thunderbird ripped a sharp turn off the Pacific Coast Highway, away from the ocean toward the heart of the heart of the continent. At that moment, Coyote was so deep in the middle of a succulent story he never noticed the turn.

Over the next few days, Coyote Woman led Coyote on an exotic adventure into profound biological, ecological and spiritual mysteries. They romped in a canyon of coastal redwoods carpeted with dripping ferns, lay back on a sawgrass hilltop scratching Venus and Mars, trotted through rows of asparagus and garlic fields, and frolicked with intoxicating sophistication among grapevines in the Sierra foothills. The enthralling beat went on, vibrating to a tuning fork planted in the planet's molten DNA, until Thunderbird slowed while climbing the High Sierra past cool mountain lakes, impossible valleys, and ridiculous trees. Suddenly, Coyote Woman became nasty as hell.

Slashing incisors and hard mirror eyes flashed Coyote a different but also quite urgent message. He slammed on the brakes and swung into an old mining road next to a tumbling mountain stream. He stopped the car and jumped out, Coyote Woman snapping at his heels. With Coyote Woman glaring and nipping, he madly tidied up the abandoned gold mine next to the stream. He rolled rocks, propped timbers, and swept with his tail. As the last tailful of dust puffed out the entrance, she stepped inside.

She fiercely hung curtains over the entrance, then pulled them closed tight, without a word. And the snows fell.

Coyote spent the winter pacing outside the cave, scraping snow off Thunderbird, running to the marmot store, checking the tires, running to the marmot store, standing in the snowfall, running to the marmot store, sleeping under the Thunderbird, running to the marmot store.

As the days lengthened, the frozen stream slowly unglued. The sun finally rose high enough to pierce the darkness at the cave entrance. Lying outside with his tail curled around him, Coyote jumped when he saw the curtains pulled open for the first time in months and a collection of bright yellow eyes peering out at him from the darkness. Before he could focus, not to mention count them all, they pounced, covering him with roughhousing furballs. "Dad," they yipped, "let's play ball."

Chapter 2
Coyote Walks the Kids

"OK, let's go," Coyote said, and stepped out the door.

Outside flowers were yellow, flowers were red, flowers were blue in the mountain gardens. "A beautiful summer day," he said out loud, but nobody was listening.

Around his feet were clumps of racing and scuffling dust, clouds of surliness, snatches of disdain, flashes of rhetoric. They raced around boulders and up trees and down holes.

How many Little Coyotes were there? Coyote didn't know.

Coyote Woman had counted, he remembered that. How many did she say? He couldn't remember. And he couldn't keep track. They were already all over the place.

Coyote was proud as a grizzly but harried as a rabbit by this turn of events. The Coyote family needed more territory, that much was clear. Not nearly enough marmot stew to go around what with all the mountain lions and toothless gold rush grandchildren and aging hippies and defeated ski bums fighting over every scrap. Where does this highway lead? Coyote wondered. I'd better find out.

He stuffed all the furballs into the waiting Thunderbird. Coyote children tumbled over the front seats, grabbed the gearshift, swung on the wheel, played with the rearview mirror, and dug busily at the upholstery. "Hey, that's real Naugahyde," snarled Coyote.

He hoisted Baby Coyote up onto his shoulders. She was soft as a roll of toilet paper. She wore a fluffy dress and shoes shaped like bunnies. She was the mistress of the tenacious hug. She whispered into his ear, "Bunnies. I want to see bunnies."

"OK," said Coyote, "I'll show you bunnies," as she pulled on his ears. He pulled the Thunderbird onto the highway and began to roll down the mountain.

"Where are we going? Where are we going?" yipped the scuffling furballs around him.

"What?" said Coyote.

"Where we going?"

The kids were growing up, that much was clear, thought Coyote. Entertaining them was getting to be impossible. What could a father think to do?

As he drove, he was thinking about how nice Baby Coyote felt clinging to his neck. He was thinking about what a refreshing afternoon it was. He was thinking about a trip to terrorize some public park in Reno. The kids could monopolize the slide, chase flashers, bob for goldfish, eat squirrels.

Up ahead a big truck was laboring down the steep grade, its brakes smoking. As Coyote pulled in behind, he slowed down enough to read a colorful billboard flowing by. It showed pictures of strange animals and bright lights and cotton candy.

OK. They could always go to the State Fair.

Coyote's Thunderbird was covered with Little Coyote bodies as it idled in a huge traffic jam somewhere near the fairgrounds. Children were in the trunk and in the glove compartment and in the ashtrays. Baby Coyote was clinging to his neck, whispering in his ear, "Bunnies. I want to see bunnies."

He took a quick U-turn to the first sign he saw out of the corner of his eye indicating PARKING. He thought he heard something from a few of the Little Coyotes about one or two falling off, but he had to keep moving. Traffic was ferocious. Parking was impossible.

PARKING turned out to be on somebody's lawn. A woman the size of a freight train engine was motioning drivers desperate from carloads of screaming kids onto her lawn, at which point she charged them five bucks for the privilege. Coyote parked and paid. Gladly. The Little Coyotes had already chewed holes in the upholstery and broken off the rearview mirror.

Baby Coyote hung onto his neck. Little Coyotes hopped onto skateboards and roller skates and into each other's pockets. Others streaked around pissing on tires.

"Meet me here at five o'clock," Coyote announced. "Here. At the Thunderbird. Nowhere else. Don't get lost. Got that?"

Nodding. Pulling. Scratching. Pissing. Farting. Disappearing.

The huge freight train woman smiled. Coyote noticed that her cowcatcher teeth appeared to be filed into points.

They crossed the street and entered the fairgrounds.

"House of Horrors! House of Horrors!" yipped the ecstatic Little Coyotes.

A huge steamy moat surrounded a mock Victorian house. Amplified screams filled the air. The mouth of an eagle formed the door. "Oh, oh," thought Coyote. "Better not go in there!" he shouted.

Too late. A pack of Little Coyotes had already raced in. They emerged minutes later with their fur standing on end, draped in body parts and blood. Rubber body parts and washable blood, for the most part. They loved it, of course. Except Coyote had a nagging suspicion that more coyotes went in than came out.

Baby Coyote pulled his ears. "Cotton candy, cotton candy!" OK, OK. He bought a big fluffy cone and handed it up. She had to learn the truth about cotton candy on her own.

"Yuck," she said, and dropped the sugar fur onto his head. "I agree," he said, taking it and pulling off a pawful. Little Coyotes tore at the cotton candy before it hit the trash barrel. They all agreed that it was vile.

"And no rides," said Coyote. "Rides will make you sick."

Up ahead a sign flashed. Bumper cars? Coyote didn't know fairs had bumper cars. Coyote used to be good at bumper cars. Coyote bought tickets and the whole Coyote crew hopped in and drove like fiends. Baby Coyote hung on like a flea as Coyote bashed and backed up with the best of them. All the drivers behaved like junkies, with glassy stares and possessed grins. This was the Coyote School of Driver Training. Some Little Coyotes jumped out to chase tires—"Don't do that!" yelled Coyote, too late, as deep blue haloes of electricity crackled around them.

"No more rides after this. No way," said Coyote.

"Ice cream cone," said the gentle voice above him who could do no wrong. OK, OK. He bought a double dipper fair special slathered in chocolate and strawberries and nuts and whipped cream.

They entered a barn full of chickens. "Now this is great stuff," drooled Coyote. The Littlest Coyote pulled his ears. "Bunnies, I want to see bunnies," she said. A wad of whipped cream fell on his nose.

"These are bunnies," drooled Coyote.

After that they looked at the dairy bunnies, the thoroughbred bunnies, the draft horse bunnies, and the pork bunnies.

"I want to see bunnies," said his ears, now stuck to his head with ice cream cement, while the remaining Little Coyotes scattered to run under the hooves of huge draft horses and gnaw the ankles of 2,000 pound bulls and trade insults with multicolored punk chickens.

Instead, Coyote hit the bright flashing lights of the Midway. How he wanted to see the Biggest Snake in the World, the Smallest Horse in the World, the Fattest Man in the World, the Three-Headed Woman, all gathered in one place at one time. And all of them in the *Guinness Book of World Records*! Amazing. The Little Coyotes yipped "rip-off" and dashed off to ride the Hungry Hawk Daredevil Speedflyer. "I don't think that's a good idea," thought Coyote. Too late.

"Bunnies," said his ears. "I want to see bunnies."

"OK, I'll show you bunnies," said Coyote, and bought tickets for the Ferris wheel. Up high over the raucous Midway, high over the jams and jellies, high over the nearby city and suburbs, high over the ranches and desert and mountains and lakes and forests and coasts, high into the soft white puffs of cloud they rode. Baby Coyote looked up and saw a soft white cloud with ears and paws and a puff of tail. "Bunny!" she said. Coyote looked down. What he saw made him sick.

No Little Coyotes were anywhere in sight. He looked at the hot dog stands and the hot pepper stands and the hot tamale stands and the french fry stands and the fresh lemonade stands and the House of Horrors and the Hungry Hawk and the Bounty Hunter and the Sideshow and the Sheep Rancher. He looked outside the entrance where the red Thunderbird was gleaming on the lawn. No one. Only the huge bloated woman, waving in more cars and picking her teeth with a pool cue.

The clock on the State Fair tower read 5:00 PM. Back at the Thunderbird the freight train woman grinned with exhaustion, her bulges consuming several lawn chairs. Had she seen any Little Coyotes? She shook her massive head. And belched tiny tufts that looked like fur.

Coyote and Baby Coyote drove home. The freeways were jammed with people going to spend the night at the fair. "At least I still have you," Coyote said, as he felt her light weight on his neck, her paws clinging to his ears. "Bunnies," she said.

Back home, Coyote and Baby Coyote parked the car and walked toward the curtains of the cave. "Bunnies!" she said, pointing up.

Coyote looked up. White puffs of clouds now outlined in gold drifted against a magenta sunset sky. And the clouds looked like bunnies. Real bunnies, each one slowly hopping across the sky.

"OK," said Coyote, "I'll show you bunnies." He held her high over his head. She smiled a huge smile. He threw her up into the air. She giggled. He threw her higher and she laughed out loud. He threw her higher still, up over the trees, and she laughed and laughed, the tears rolling down her delighted cheeks.

He threw her higher still. High up she soared, a little ball of fluff, high up in the light mountain air, reaching toward the clouds, touching the clouds.

And the bunnies paused. They watched her coming. One large white cloud reached out a soft white forepaw and caught her and put her on its neck, slowly gathered its feet together and floated out again across the evening sky.

Coyote waited. He lay on his back and looked up at the clouds, now darkening and colliding overhead. He yipped. He howled. He cried.

And he yipped, he howled, he cried.

He lay there and watched and waited as the sky cracked open and rain came down and flowed over him, as bunnies dropped from the sky in buckets and hopped away, as his heart broke and ran salt tears down into the stream and into the river and down, down, down to mix with the saltwater sea.

No joke. No laughing matter. Coyote had lost them all.

Chapter 3
Coyote Travels Around

"They'll turn up. They always do," Coyote Woman said as she jumped into the Thunderbird.

Thunderbird peeled back onto the mountain freeway, wheeling down the east side of the Sierra Nevada, Coyote at the wheel, Coyote Woman next to him, riding shotgun, building up speed, rolling toward Reno. But just then Earthquake Man groaned with indigestion and rolled over on his magma bed, shaking his tattered California covers and flailing this green highway Interstate 80 engineering marvel like an umbilical cord. *Craaack!!! Snaaap!!!* went the interstate. *Bwanggg!* went the Thunderbird as it launched off the undulating ribbon of concrete into the desert air. Coyote hung on tight to the wheel, but Coyote Woman bounced out, tumbling into the thundering roadside dust.

Watching in the rearview mirror, Coyote saw her disappear into a cloud as Thunderbird flew on toward the eastern horizon.

"We'll be seeing you, Coyote Man!" Coyote Woman howled as she rolled to a stop in a drainage ditch within the city limits of Reno, Nevada, where she is still remembered today as a keeper of motel secrets and a sharp dealer in instant dreams.

Coyote and the Thunderbird didn't stop flying until they hit the peaks of the Rocky Mountains somewhere near Independence Pass in a land of gestating mountains and rivers without end.

Whammm!

Coyote lay behind the wheel a long time, paw prints of dust poofing through his flying mind. Finally he threw his head back and yipped into the night air filled with the moon rising big as a silver fried egg. He yipped and howled all night, his back killing him, his heart bouncing like a baby on a trampoline, his stomach rumbling, his breath visible. "Aiee," he wailed, "my family is ground to dust by Earthquake and I am all alone! What am I to do?"

"Well, first things first." At dawn, he and Thunderbird went fishing.

The Thunderbird was wedged between towering boulders next to a deep mountain pool straddling the Continental Divide feeding a stream tumbling east, no west, no east, no west. Coyote perched on the hood and dangled a piece of string over the dark shadows, flicked it, jerked it. "Come on" he said to the cold water, fresh snowmelt, glacier clear, thin blue sky, rising yellow sun, "Come on, baby, come to Coyote, gonna get me the Big One, ten-thousand-year-old mother of every Rainbow Trout on the continent, a smart one."

"What do you like, Trout Mother?" crooned Coyote, tossing in flies expertly tied with pieces of whisker, then real flies, then worms, grasshoppers and old french fries dipped in ketchup he found under the driver's seat.

Nothing. Not a bite. Not a nibble. "Damn," said Coyote, "this is not working."

He lay on the sun-warmed hood of the car and thought. He tied his line to the grille so that it dangled into the pool and put his head down on his paws to think some more. The sheet metal hood felt so warm and contoured and elegant in the sun, Coyote fell asleep. He dreamed.

"Try this then," said Coyote. He gathered up pastel wildflowers, tied them with a bow of aspen bark, placed them in a stone pitcher on a pine table casually strewn with environmental newsletters plus a fresh copy of the morning paper. He added two colorful cloth kerchief napkins, a fresh pot of coffee, and two cinnamon rolls each flanked by two eggs over easy plus crisp bacon. He laid it all out on the table for two next to the Thunderbird above the shadowy pool, then called out, "Breakfast time, Trout Mother!" while carrying the table down over the sharp boulders, ouch ouch, *down to the*

rim of the icy pool, steadied it on the rocks, put his paw in the glacial water, aieee, *jerked it out, saw a giant ripple in the pool, then a wave, then color flare out from the shadows.*

Coyote quickly sat down at the dry-side place setting, snapped open the newspaper, scanned the sports page and read the comics while a huge lantern-lipped flash of rainbow spots lolled to the surface, broke the surface tension, took a fat real fly. Coyote sipped the coffee, ouch, too hot, thinking come on, come to me Trout Mother, come on.

Trout Mother glided silently toward the table, her slick body flashing in the sun. Coyote scanned and sipped as she rolled up to the breakfast lure and opened her huge raspy jaws. Oh, oh, thought Coyote, still reading but watching out of the corner of his eye. She reached for the coffee, then the editorials. Then the cinnamon roll. Then the advice columns. A half-hour later, she spoke. "How many miles you got on that thing?" she asked, glancing at the Thunderbird.

They talked well into the afternoon. Lost parent talk. Mountain talk. Running water talk. Trout Mother passed along tips on child rearing and designs for small-scale hydro projects and her granola recipe. When she had polished off the last of the eggs, coffee, and roll, she wiped her jaws with the napkin. "Here's my card," she said. "Call me anytime. As for finding the kids, I'll leave directions." Coyote stuffed the card into his kit bag. When he looked up, she was gone.

Coyote woke. The sun was passing out of sight below him in the west. The huge ragged black shadow of the

Rockies spread out to the mysterious east in front of him. The waters of the pool were still and black and cold. He reeled in his line. His fly was gone. In its place was a fresh wildflower bouquet. And a note. But the handwriting was blurred. He couldn't tell if it said, "Go west, young man," or "east."

At sunrise Coyote pushed the Thunderbird into nascent ruts running along the apex of the Continental Divide. Coyote hopped in and let the Thunderbird decide which direction to go. It rolled... east down the mountain, Coyote and Thunderbird building up speed down rocky crags and through black tunnels and over round foothills and into thick smog, *cough cough*, past sprawling cities and finally out into oceanic plains with windmills for trees. Where am I? thought Coyote.

That night Coyote and the Thunderbird rolled off Interstate 80, bumping to a stop in a county park under a bank of cottonwoods next to a river running placid and thin as a silver ribbon in the moonlight.

As he reached into his kit bag for his toothbrush, out fell Trout Mother's business card. Surprised, he held it up to the moon's eye. On one side was a reproduction of a rainbow billboard he remembered seeing several times along the mountain highways. "Get your Power from Mountain Hydro," it read. The other side gave her 800 number. The card was slick with fish oil. "I will definitely have to give that number a call," thought Coyote.

He curled up next to the riverbank and fell asleep just as the dawn light broke over the Great Plains and decorated the spiders' webs with dewy deposits of diamonds. A tendril of morning breeze lifted Trout Mother's card out of Coyote's sleeping paw. It floated out over the impossibly shallow stream, then settled on the surface. The fish oil card worked its way easily into the soft current. In a stroke of its powerful tail, it was gone.

The stream eventually became the Platte, then the Missouri, then the Mississippi, the huge-veined heart of North America.

The next day Coyote and Thunderbird lead-footed it with excited curiosity through a thousand miles of frying pan flat country east past dancing sandhill cranes and tan fields colored with pronghorns to greener fields with crops tall and taller and then forests taller and wetter still as Thunderbird turned north. Thunderbird didn't slow until he reached Highway 61, which scratches the nose of the huge wolf's head of freshwater called Lake Superior. Coyote sneezed with delight, the bottomless giant lake and the tall white pines so turned him on.

He camped a few miles off the highway in a white pine grove on a bed of pine needles. Coyote settled in, so soft, so quiet, the pine scent wafting through his nostrils like a perfume sampler. He curled up under the warm mufflers of the Thunderbird and instantly fell asleep. He dreamed.

He dreamed that a magnificent white pine spread her heavy black arms over him, letting her fingers filter the starlight into soft shadows as Coyote sniffed up into the soft cleavage of limbs, sensing a comfortable home, a nest, a flicker nest freshly pecked in the huge trunk. Coyote sniffed the feathered home of fresh flicker eggs, of bleeding veins of pine xylem and phloem, just as the eggs hatched. There was a sudden explosion of flickers with whiskers and pine needles for feathers. They fanned out over the forest with raucous flicker laughter while Coyote fell softly back onto the pine boughs and fell asleep to the accordion music of Northern Lights playing through the fingernails of pines, sweet Aurora Borealis flashing a concert of spectral tunes.

In rosy-fingered first light, Coyote woke to the echo of flicker laughter. He climbed into the Thunderbird just in time to see the swoop and glide of a Flicker through the trees—a touch of red, a butt of white, a hint of yellow. A flicker feather with a yellow shaft floated out of the trees onto his nose. It had a whisker at the tip.

He tied the feather onto the rearview mirror and backed out of the grove toward the Superior coast. Pine needles rustled and Flicker laughed as Thunderbird turned northeast along the dark lake flared gold by the rising sun. Coyote sniffed the scent of pulp mills and nickel smelters as he rounded the northern tip of the Great Lakes, raced past Georgian Bay and vaulted Niagara Falls.

By the time they arrived in Florida it was midnight. Coyote and Thunderbird rolled off highway A1A into a palm-lined parking lot next to the Atlantic Ocean. The parking lot was a canyon nestled in the mountain range of high-rise condominiums that ran up and down the coast, disappearing into a haze of power plant and cruise ship smoke.

He grabbed his towel and went to sleep out on the empty beach under the full moon. He stared dreamily at the silver-plated surf rolling in from Africa in powerful rhythmic drumbeats. His heartbeat synchronized to the rhythm of the waves while his nose sniffed the moon's menstrual persuasion.

Suddenly the hair stood up on his back. Huge Paleolithic beasts were emerging from the surf and slowly, painfully making their lumbering way toward him. They came right to his pawtips, silent as stones, then laboriously flippered holes into the warm sand and laid their eggs, one after another. Coyote gazed into their round watery eyes, transfixed by their deep oceanic understanding. He guarded their nests all night while talking Turtle with Turtle Mothers up and down the beach. At dawn, exhausted, their stone heads carried his charms back to the surf and the sea.

Pooped, Coyote and Thunderbird drove away from the range of coastal condominiums past funeral homes and memorial parks and convalescent care centers and eye and liver clinics. Coyote tried to nap in a giant pharmacy parking lot but was assaulted by blue-haired ladies with dead husbands seeking conversation. They shuffled the streets on gleaming aluminum walkers, thousands of them carrying literature on tax avoidance and memories of Northern marriages and hopes of grandchildren visiting. But he couldn't accept their eager invitations. The cops told him to keep it moving—he didn't have a parking permit.

Coyote and the Thunderbird blasted west on the Keys causeway, rocketing through Key West at sunset to the cheers of contortionists, jugglers, writers, and drunks, then leaped out over the Gulf and slalomed around oil rigs. Then he slipped into New Orleans for Mardi Gras, raced Texas dust devils over a horizon of artificially-inseminated longhorns, dipped into Mexico for several fiestas, then turned North for summer state fairs and the pow wow season. Coyote was on such a roll he caught the Blood Indian Pow Wow and the Calgary Stampede and the Edmonton Megamall and the DEW Line in one weekend, then ran back through Toronto and Albany and Baltimore and Chattanooga and Des Moines and Waco and Albuquerque and Window Rock and Winnemucca and Coeur d'Alene and around and around again faster and faster. Coyote and Thunderbird were moving so fast they whirled up clouds of moisture from the Atlantic and the Gulf and the Pacific and Hudson's Bay, building up huge chortling thunderheads over North America. The clouds welled up over the continent like a smiling Godzilla with teeth of lightning and claps of thunder and winds of laughter and rains of applause.

Coyote Woman listened to the unusual weather report on her satellite radio in Reno. She knew it had to be Coyote. Only Thunderbird was so fast, only Coyote so rooted yet aimless.

The timing was right. Reno sucked, she knew that now. As the powerful Chair of Nevada's Gaming Commission, she had been unable to reform the paltry imaginations of a state full of quick-fix dream merchants and suckers. She had made her mark but couldn't beat them at their own game. She had to imagine bigger fish. Not to mention, she had the urge again to settle down

So, she called the Little Coyotes together. They had wandered back to their mountain home after spending several days sniffing around town pouncing on bugs, throwing snakes in the air, and playing video games at the arcade until their curiosity was fried. They all agreed that it was time for Coyote to slow down. They set a trap.

On the longest uphill grade on Interstate 70 in the heart of the Rocky Mountains, they placed a series of five bright-red signs on the shoulder, each with a partial line of text: "If you want to know..." "The way of birth..." "Turn right..." "Then left..." "To the center of the Earth." They knew that Coyote, a slave to curiosity, could not resist such an invitation. At the next exit, they added an orange Detour sign pointing up a winding two-track mountain road that terminated at an abandoned gold mine. Over the mine entrance they installed a green highway sign—Tunnel. Slow down. Inside, the mineshaft grew narrower and narrower. Finally, it ended. Thunderbird would have to come to a stop.

The trap was set. Coyote Woman chuckled to herself. "Slow down, Coyote," she thought to herself. "I want to show you something. It's a gold mine I own. It's deep and moist and very exciting, with real gold in it. Say, you ever thought about getting married?"

Chapter 4
Coyote Attends the Wedding

Coyote was driving along. Thunderbird was sniffing the green lines of interstate highways, then the red lines of federal highways, the blue lines of state highways, the black lines of old forgotten trunk highways, then the broken lines of unpaved two-tracks open only part of the year, unreliable, unsafe for most vehicles, not to mention a low slung '56 Thunderbird with its mufflers already torn loose and hanging on by coat hangers. Those lines were leading Coyote toward the fiery heart of America's most active volcanic mountain range. Its towering craggy peaks and deep slashing valleys had erupted out of the center of an island's granite bedrock less than three centuries before. Unpredictable, it had erupted many times since and could erupt again at any moment. Wary, his fur bristling, Coyote and Thunderbird entered the deep dark tunnel that carried them to that ferocious human caldera called New York City.

How could he have avoided it? He was following the directions on an invitation sent to the Coyote family months ago. It announced a wedding. Coyote loved weddings. Saw them as journey to the molten core at the center of the earth. Not to mention a great occasion for a party.

So of course he did everything he could to attend. Had to borrow gasoline from a closed gas station by siphoning the tanks of the tow trucks. Had to not pay the bills once neatly arranged on the table by Coyote Woman even though he had said, "I'll take care of them, don't worry about it." Had to ignore for just a few days more the leak in the roof of the Coyote lair which kept running a stream of water over the breakfast, lunch, and dinner table, damn, whenever it rained, damn. Had to leave the big rattler still coiled around the scruffy prairie rose bush in the front yard, making everybody nervous. Had to leave the bag of melon seeds lying by the steps where he had been "going out to plant them right this minute, yes I am," and instead wandered around and gathered up a whole hoard of wild asparagus, who could complain about that? But the seed bag sat by the back door for months until a Little Coyote said out loud one day how sweet and juicy those melons were going to be tasting and damn Coyote ran out and there were the seeds all sprouted in a heap. Well, Coyote was not cut out to be a farmer anyway, although he certainly was very fond of eating melons.

He had meant to tell Coyote Woman and the Little Coyotes about this wedding to which they all had been invited, but then how could they all go and still be responsible for the backyard garden which, after all, she had finally planted. Wasn't his fault. So while Coyote Woman was hanging the wash and stoking the stove and weeding the garden and the Little Coyotes were rolling in the river and flicking dragonflies and shagging gophers, he stepped out the back door to borrow a hoe from a neighbor, "Be right back," and he was gone.

As he drove down the freeway, he felt so relaxed. His mind was churning with thick black truck stop coffee, his eyes dazzled by a full panoply of barking stars. As the Thunderbird mesmerized him with the glare of oncoming headlights, he recalled his own wedding.

It was a grand affair. The birds and the beasts were there. He had been cruising the west coast in his brand new (to him) Thunderbird when she pounced full-blown into his dream. He remembered that. He remembered the smell of her hitchhiking fur and the glint of her sunset smile. He remembered fall frolics and the winter den and the surprise of Little Coyotes. He remembered losing the Little Coyotes to the fair and Baby Coyote to a cloud and spousal separation by Earthquake. But she tracked him down with her satellite dish and laid a clever mind-hold trap for him in the mountains. She invited all his friends to the ceremony including Trout Mother and Turtle Woman and White Pine and Flicker and lured the mythical Thunderbird itself by disguising a mineshaft as an interstate highway tunnel. And there in the darkness, deep in the warm center of the earth, Thunderbird and Coyote finally rolled to a stop and—surprise!—corks popped, root beer foamed, crepe paper crinkled, and the crowd buzzed with excitement and Coyote wondered "What the...?" But there she was smiling in the headlights wearing a long flowered satin dress with the Little Coyotes dancing excitedly next to her, sniffing and peeing. He squeezed out of the seat and stepped up next to her and they were married on the spot to the music of water dripping and drummers drumming and flickers laughing and turtles digging and white pine sighing and Trout Mother presiding under Thunderbird's double headlight grin.

That was years ago. Now there are Little Coyotes as far as the eye can see and the nose can distinguish the scent of humor in concentrations as low as three parts per million. More and more of them all the time, turning up everywhere, city, mountain, country, desert, spreading the Gospel According to Coyote like wild rice and fry bread, like peanut butter and jelly, like cream cheese and bagels, like pork hocks and collard greens, like fiery chiles and refried beans, spreading it across the continent without regard to race, religion, creed, color, genus, or species.

Coyote awoke a married man. As he drove, he stole another glance at the invitation in his lap.

THE PLEASURE OF YOUR COMPANY
IS REQUESTED AT THE MARRIAGE
OF THE *SAND* AND THE *REED*.

NEW YORK CITY.
THE DATE. THE TIME. THE PLACE.

The Sand and the Reed. He sensed the elegance of such a union. He vibrated to the appropriateness of it. His fur rustled with the wind that animated it. The sand and the reed were to marry, anchoring the reed in the sand, the reed holding the sand in place. A perfect symbiosis. Coyote had to be there. He couldn't wait.

Coyote had hit the river tunnels during the early morning rush hour of a clear blue day and disappeared into horn honking and carbon monoxide and night. He emerged from the birth tunnel rubbing his startled eyes as Thunderbird floated and bucked down grand canyons of cars and eddied into exotic side canyons and arroyos shaped and scoured by immigrants, all the time buzzed and harassed by untold swarms of angry black and yellow bees. Thunderbird eventually pulled up, frantic and exhausted, in front of an elegant spire emerging from deep shadows between towering high-rises. Coyote stared at the address. This was the place. He checked his watch. Now was the time.

The sun at high noon penetrated the canyon and struck the stained-glass church and turned it into an explosion of blinding colored lights.

Coyote pushed through the reflected rainbow light and entered a cool dark interior, as the doors closed behind him. The darkness was so sudden he was momentarily blinded. He could only hear and smell and taste. He heard the quiet rustling of reeds and the eternal shifting of sands. He smelled the aromas of perfume and flowers and the wetness and pungency of love. The primordial taste of marriage exploded on his tongue. The hair stood up all over his body.

His eyes grew wider in the darkness, his pupils as big as cyclones. He made out a larger circle of guests containing a smaller circle of attendants. He saw the beauty of the attendants and his knees turned to water and he thought, I hope there will be dancing at the reception. I am so careless I should have asked. But of course there will be, this is a wedding. The attendants faced each other, each dressed as a flower. And they all suddenly opened, as one flower would open, a giant amaryllis opening at the moment its genes and its gestation insisted it must. And inside the center petals were the Sand and the Reed. Coyote was dazzled.

Coyote was surprised as well to note that one of the attendants was none other than the resplendent flower of Coyote Woman. And as his eyes widened, he was shocked to see that the circle of guests contained the numerous lazy furred ears of the Little Coyotes. They were everywhere.

He could stand it no longer. He tilted back his head. He flattened his ears. He howled his arrival. He howled his joy.

Chapter 5
The Origin of Fall

By mid-September, the Coyote family needed to cool off. The Midwest's summer furnace was still red hot and furious, offering up a last blast of towering inferno heat and humidity before the soft palette of rust and golden harvest commenced. The Coyote Lair was roasting.

So Tornado came. Tornado came as if in a dream. Quiet. Sleepy. No flashing of night lightning. No beating of night rain. Just a sick yellow pastel sky and clouds piled high as a giant's top hat. Out of the west it came, tall and black and writhing its hips like a snake oil woman, then roaring like a Fee-Fi-Fo-Fum giant smelling the blood and fur of the Coyote family.

Coyote was caught by surprise. He ran around fast as he could to undo the whirlwind but too late. Tornado hit the Coyote Lair like a ton of bricks, fell on the Coyote

Lair like a black tarpaulin of wind and water, cracked and smashed and crushed and imploded the Coyote Lair like a kid stomping an ant's nest, like the Great Exterminator stomping a household of roaches. Then it was gone.

Coyote woke up in the quiet, with only the train whistle guitar of tornado twisting out of earshot in the distance. Coyote found himself hanging by his tail from a spread-eagled oak, the iron branches flexing fingerless arms to the sick raining sky. Coyote untangled himself and looked around.

The lair was shot, that was clear. That's OK, it wasn't much anyway. Just some particleboard panels nailed together forming the entry to an old Airstream trailer he had scored at the auction of a formerly prosperous farmer's stash of ace stuff.

Still, Coyote was sad about the Airstream. He remembered fondly the day the family moved in.

The Coyote family was driving along, everybody hanging over the sides of the Thunderbird enjoying the sunset air along a dusty road through fields of giant sunflowers nodding to them on both sides. They came upon a dust cloud generated by cars peeling out in front of a scrawled Auction Today sign tacked to a fence post next to a side road winding deep into the sunflowers. They had to investigate.

"Ooohhh," they all said when they saw it. For some reason the gleaming Airstream next to the unpainted barn next to the peeling house in the grove of trees hadn't sold

all day. When the Coyote family drove up everybody had packed up. The auctioneer was hoarse. The moon was rising. They got a steal.

The kids were excited. They were feeling a bit constricted in the Thunderbird's two seats, a sure sign of growing up. Coyote hitched up the Airstream and wheeled down the gravel road like a silver moonbeam. But the tires went flat and the suspension collapsed just a mile down the road. All the Coyotes got out and looked around. Their radiant moonbeam home collapsed on the shoulder of County Road X next to a river running through a one-school town.

"Well," said Coyote, "this looks like a good spot. Let's live here for a while." They dragged the trailer into the grass along the riverbank and propped it up on mossy concrete blocks hauled from the river. It's been parked there ever since, people stopping by all the time asking, "How do you like the Airstream?" "Fine," said Coyote, kicking the flat tires. Coyote Woman thought it sucked, but the Little Coyotes liked it.

Wait a minute! thought Coyote. The Little Coyotes, where are they??? Coyote Woman, where is she???

Not a murmur. Not a yip or cry. Coyote dug under the shiny stainless panels of the shattered Airstream. Nothing. Coyote dug under the tacky particleboard entrance panels. Nothing. Nothing at all.

"Aieee!" wailed Coyote. "What am I to do? My wife and children have been vaporized by Tornado. What am I to do?"

"Oh well," he said, drawing a breath, "they'll turn up. They always do." And he trotted off toward town.

The small town (tornadoes always strike small towns) was abuzz with tornado talk. The tornado had passed near the outskirts, terrifying school children and giving numerous ham radio operators something to do but causing no injuries. The back porch of the Odegaard place had been ripped off, but they'd been meaning to do that anyway. The Clovis' barn had imploded and that was bad news because now there's hay and dead pigs all over the messed-up place, but they were insured.

Coyote yipped, "The Clovis' place? The Clovis' place? Misfortune at the Clovis' place?" He could not believe his good fortune. Weak in the knees from the mere mention of the Clovis moniker, Coyote quickly reached into his kit bag for an appropriate disguise. In a second he was transformed into a Courteous Helpful Friendly Insurance Agent from the Home Office. "Hello," he practiced, "I'm here to help the Clovis family recover from their loss as quickly as possible. Can you show me to your delightful daughter...I mean, the scene of the slaughter?"

No, he meant delightful daughter. Secretly Coyote had had his eye on Mavis, the Clovis eldest daughter, but Coyote Woman kept him on a tight leash. He was always hauling water, chopping wood, stacking the dishes, setting the table, cutting the grass, fixing the Thunderbird. Coyote attended endless PTA meetings and teacher's conferences to keep the Little Coyotes in school, despite the deep and abiding objections of the principal who had had it with the little buggers after only three days of the first grade. Coyote never seemed to have any time for any fun.

But occasionally Coyote managed to steal a glimpse of the fabulously ripening plum on the town streets called Mavis Clovis. What a number. She moved like a sack of oiled ball bearings. Her hair, one day dark, one day light, was tangled with wanton insouciance. Her eyes had eager towns-males standing stupefied in the street. And her lips. One day those fat pouts, those uplifted curls, would bring kissing back full-bore to the silver screen. The strong fetched her Cokes or firewood as gifts. The weak stood stock still, knees melted and fused.

For four straight years she had played the lead in the high school play. In the previous eighty years of town history, the audience for school plays consisted entirely of the cast members' nervous moms and tired dads and restless brothers and jealous sisters. But during the four years of the Mavis Clovis epoch the auditorium at County X High School was crammed with farmers and dishwashers and bankers and hardware store managers from the entire county. Nothing on TV that night could compete. Coyote Woman, who had a penchant for theater, nevertheless managed not to allow Coyote away from home those nights, although lately he bought tickets a year in advance. The children have too much homework, said Coyote Woman, polishing her teeth with a dishtowel.

Only once had he managed to catch Mavis Clovis alone. She was wandering along the quiet riverbank outside of town memorizing her lines—"Midsummer Night's Dream" meets "Cat on a Hot Tin Roof." From his backyard, he sniffed her on the downwind breeze. Coyote tiptoed down to the riverbank, then slalomed upstream through the red willows like a Pentagon General's fantasy rocket. He found her pacing under a tree.

He offered to help her with her lines. She agreed. Marilyn Monroe meets Joe DiMaggio. Then he made up his own stories—one after another—so he could continue to smell her ripening.

She liked his stories, she said, and wanted to come back for more. He'd try, he said, and God knows he meant it. But it was tough. The whole world was watching, or so it seemed. Tornado gave him the chance to try again.

He carefully knocked on the Clovis' front door, which he noted was punctured with pieces of straw fired through it like arrows by Tornado. The door creaked open. "Good afternoon, ma'am. I'm from the Local Farmers' Home Insurance office, here to assess the damage and get you the fastest insurance restitution in the Western Hemisphere so that you and your family can be back on your feet in no time. I'd like to meet with all members of the family to see what can be done for you immediately."

Mrs. Clovis eyed him suspiciously. She was as big as the shattered barn and tough as boiled owls from her years of tossing hay bales and mixing dough balls and throwing scumbag suitors of her daughter Mavis off the front porch as far as the nearby creek (where many of them to this day lay face down in the mud stone-dead). Did she recognize him? After all, he had been there once or twice before, maybe ten or twenty times, in ten or twenty different disguises, checking after the Clovis' health, the rain gutters, the siding, repairing tractors, renting combines, offering artificial insemination for the sows, whatever it took to mount a serious assault on Mavis Clovis' charms.

But the sadistic Mrs. Clovis saw through his disguises every time—sometimes immediately, more often than not after he had performed some useful task or another—and threw him off the porch toward the creek. Flying through the air he went, disguises and wrenches, or hammers and nails, or salesman's notebooks, or artificial insemination kits flying with him. "Aieeee," he'd sing, limping all the way home, where Coyote Woman looked at him with a jaundiced eye.

This time his disguise seemed to work. Mrs. Clovis had tearful red runny eyes that clearly impaired her vision. Not to mention this had to be Coyote's best disguise to date. The stiff chalk-striped suit. The rep tie pulled tight at the collar, fastidiously refusing to accommodate the intense heat, the killer humidity. The leatherette briefcase filled with valuable forms and documents. The painful black wingtips.

The wingtips were the clincher. Coyote, for all his disguises, was seriously into comfort. Meaning that he would usually neglect the proper footwear for his disguise, as tight shoes drove him nuts. Usually he wore sneakers. Or moccasins. Maybe sandals. But that was as far as he would go. So the wingtips today were the perfect detail. There was no stopping him now. As he took out his notebook and poised his pen, the perspiration that dripped on it could reasonably have been attributed to the thick fetid air as to the blazing red eyes of Mrs. Clovis scanning him up and down.

"Please come in," she said, weeping. "You will hear our tale of mistreatment at the hand of Tornado."

Coyote beamed, "Please assemble your entire family so that they can describe in detail the full extent of the tragedy."

Coyote sat in the living room of the asphalt shingle-sided farmhouse with the windows covered with blasted hay bales and melting pig parts. The living room was understandably small. After all, there were only fourteen members of the family. Thirteen of them sat on the overstuffed chairs and couches that filled the room, leaving only a small square of throw rug in the center, which is where Coyote sat on a hard metal folding chair filling notebooks one after another with inventories of woe.

Mrs. Clovis went on, "...then there was the prize Duroc, Esmeralda, who always produced fourteen piglets a litter if she produced one, didn't she Brucie? Didn't she, children? And she was recently inseminated with the frozen—ahem—of the World Champion Duroc, the AI man guaranteed me a litter of World Champions, and you know how much *they* are worth...."

It was hot. It was humid. The storm had barely passed over the horizon. The whole region was sweating profusely. And Coyote was becoming hysterical. Mavis was not there. Where was she? Where could she have been? Why wasn't she home when he needed her? His suit was itching. His shirt was pouring rivers of perspiration out the sleeves, dripping into pools on the floor as he scribbled down the virtues of boar after boar, sow after sow, piglet after piglet. "My, Mr. and Mrs. Clovis," Coyote's voice scratched out, "I had no idea you had such a large pig operation."

And his feet were killing him. His tender pouncing paws, the very paws that could keep a beach ball spinning in the air at Malibu while juggling seventeen bananas and shuffling cards with his ears in Vegas, these very talented hind paws were pressed into the unnatural black vises of leather-soled wingtips and of course he needed wool socks to make them look exactly right, all crammed into the space properly reserved for a family of small mice. And she was not here.

"And Phil the Hampshire...Honey, don't forget Phil the State Champion Hampshire Boar, won the blue ribbon he did just last summer, ribbon blew away too, saw it go, hung the plaques and ribbons on a board in the barn, full too, had to get another board for all the ribbons, damn that Phil made me proud..." Mr. Clovis went on, catching on to the game, damn him, even embellishing on it, making it hard for Coyote to breathe.

Suddenly little Jennifer, fourteen years old and riddled with erupting acne, asked out loud, "What about the sheep? Doesn't anybody care about the sheep I've been raising just so I could get them ready for this year's State Fair where my Ag instructor assured me I was going to win?" "Ahh, good point, Jenny," salivated Mrs. Clovis. "Clearly you have suffered psychological damage as well."

"Look," said Coyote, barely able to scratch the syllable out of his burned dry throat, "I get the impression that your loss was far greater than my company had anticipated." Yes, yes, yes, nodded twenty-six eyes surrounding Coyote. Yes indeed, belched thirteen mouths at the insurance man's sympathetic assertion. And don't you dare consider that we are not going to get all of our loss back to re-outfit our family in the prize pig (and sheep) business! Don't you dare! threatened a circle of raised eyebrows. And Mavis' brows weren't there, and her eyes weren't there, and her lips weren't there. Those eyes! Those lips! Where could she be!?!

At which point his polyester underwear began to melt.

"I'll have to call my District Office," Coyote said.

“The phone’s right here,” said Mrs. Clovis, handing him the fat black receiver, putting it on his lap, strafing his hand with her soaked handkerchief and razor nails. “Please do call. I’d love to hear you tell them the depth of our despair.”

“Speaking of tragedy,” Coyote mustered the courage to comment, “I notice that our records indicate that you have twelve children, and I only notice eleven of the cute little buggers in the room today. Are you missing a child?”

His words set off a storm of wailing on the part of Mr. and Mrs. Clovis, and shouts and recriminations on the part of the children, elevating the temperature in the room to near the boiling point. “The little tramp,” rasped Mr. Clovis, “She’s run off!” “Yes, run off,” echoed Mrs. Clovis, “and if I ever get my hands on that slimeball Coyote I am going to skin him alive...one hair at a time!” Jennifer piped up, “Ha ha, run to New York, to New York with Coyote, *niah niah*.”

“Why, there must be some mistake,” said Coyote, embarrassed for using such a hackneyed line but his shirt collar was now soaked and shrinking around his neck, beginning to choke him to death. “A mistake!” thundered Mrs. Clovis, raising her three hundred pounds out of her chair and towering over her Friendly Insurance Representative from the Local Office. “He’s had his slanted yellow eyes on her for years. And oftentimes she threatened to run off with him. Yesterday she did!!!” She thrust a greasy note in Coyote's simple, helpful, friendly, courteous but nevertheless completely bedraggled and now barely able to mask astonishment Insurance Man's face. Coyote read:

Dear Mommy and Daddy (as for the rest of the vermin around here, no comment):

He offered me my chance, and I'm taking it. Hollywood. But first New York. Where he has the most contacts. He says I have that 'certain something,' a 'quality' that can be a 'presence' on Broadway, then the silver screen.

No more hogs for me. No more toting bales. No more hog bad breath. No more high school. And no more of you!

And as for Coyote...

Love,

Mavis

PS I'll write when I'm famous.

God, thought Coyote, I would never use such trite lines as those. Clearly some low-level lothario—probably that new drama teacher from Fargo—has scooped up my prize, not to mention my reputation.

"First my daughter, now my pigs," wailed Mrs. Clovis. "If I ever see that Coyote again, I'll...."

Coyote saw little opportunity to clear up the confusion in the present circumstances. And he himself was not comforted by the contents of the letter. His heart was broken, no question about it. Time to save the rest of him.

He eyed the door. It was blocked by the gentle Mrs. Clovis, who, in spite of the redness of her eyes, had him directly in her sights.

"Call," she said. "I want to hear what the District Office has to say."

His feet curled up in the prison of black wingtips, his body dehydrated to a wisp under the humid breath of the thirteen Clovis mouths, his will razored into a narrow crack by the intense conspiratorial stares of the twenty-six beady Clovis eyes, Coyote slowly reached for the phone, its black rotary dial spinning in his mind into the shape of a terminal tornado, faster and faster, becoming the eye of a black hole into which he was about to be cast and crushed and lost in time.

Just then the phone rang. Coyote picked it up, his voice squeaking a weak, high-pitched falsetto hello. The voice on the other end churned with bright familiarity.

"Hello, Mrs. Clovis? This is Coyote Woman. I know it's odd for me to be calling you, Mrs. Clovis, but I was just down in the Cities scoring a few good deals at The Liquidators, you know the place, I'm sure, everybody goes there, and dropping off the Little Coyotes to have a few adventures (and frankly, let's face it, I may have had a few adventures myself if you know what I mean. Who wouldn't want to sail to Catalina for a few days with a blue-eyed sailmaker, I ask you?) but now I'm back and I find our place wrecked, that's the good news, and Coyote nowhere to be found, that may be the better news, but I need to talk to him to find out, let's face it, what the heck is going on. The people in town said they saw him heading out toward your place wearing a ridiculous suit and tie and even wingtips (dumb for a hot day like this if you ask me). The only thing I can figure is that he's looking to ogle your daughter Mavis again but everybody knows she's split for New York—or is it Hollywood?—with that new drama teacher from Fargo, so I thought I might reach him there and let him know I'm back. Is he nearby?"

As she talked, Coyote felt a breeze, crisp as apples, curl around the Clovis household and penetrate the asphalt siding and the cracked windows and the hay bales stacked around the foundation. It ruffled his fur. It cooled and dried the air instantly. Outside, the green drained out of the trees, leaving them rustling palettes of bright yellow, burnt umber, and rust. Beaver and raccoon and squirrel and porcupine and bear and frog and salamander and snake began to pack it in, call it a year. The daisies died, the asters bloomed, and the sumac wrote STOP in bold red flourishes across the hillsides. Pumpkins began to roll. Fall had begun.

And Coyote was suddenly cool as a cucumber. "That's wonderful news," Coyote said into the cradle of the receiver as he hung up.

"That was the District Office," Coyote reported, coolly rising and making his way to the door. "Your check is in the mail."

Chapter 6
Coyote Camps Out

"Aieeeee! What a day I am having already," said Coyote to himself as he spilled toothpaste all over his feet and realized that he was starving to death. "After Tornado, why did I think that a camping trip with the Little Ones was such a good idea?"

Of course, he hadn't thought it was a good idea. Coyote Woman thought it was a good idea. "Take the kids on vacation. This mess Tornado made needs to be cleaned up," she grinned.

Indeed, it did. The Coyote family's crushed Airstream was quickly condemned and swept up by bulldozers, the fractured furniture put on the roadside and picked up by scavengers. Meanwhile, Coyote Woman left town with a sailor from the Cities with a sixty-foot yacht poised on Catalina Island to cross the Pacific to Polynesian atolls.

How did Coyote know all this? The answering machine remained intact. "See you, scumbag," said the recorded voice of Coyote Woman as he stood in the phone booth at the camping supply store. "The house is gone. The garden picked. Don't wait up for me. I've always wanted to visit Polynesia. The Little Ones know how to reach me if they need to."

Making matters worse, the Little Coyotes had taken intrafamilial friction to new heights. Their relentless scuffling had reached white heat, nearly killing each other as they felled trees around the campsite and prompting more than one visit by the Department of Natural Resources police boat.

When the kids couldn't stand each other any longer, they split toward the road back to civilization, each going a separate way, of course, none of them having the slightest idea of where civilization was (not to mention what it was).

In the meantime, local bears responded with utmost dispatch this very morning to the aroma of Coyote frying up his personal stash of thick-sliced hickory smoked pepper-coated breakfast bacon, strolled up to the campsite and eyed the bacon, just drying on a paper towel. They waited for it to cool just a bit, then swiped the whole rasher. "Hey!" said Coyote. "Yeah?" said the bears, picking their teeth with very large claws. Then they shuffled off into the bush carrying the entire backpack of canned goods as well.

So, Coyote brushed his teeth and reviewed the situation.

Week one of the camping trip has been a disaster, he recorded. I can hardly wait for week two.

The sun had now emerged from the horizon of white pine and aspen. The placid lake in front of the campsite lay like a huge pool of silver flecked with gold to his doorstep (the wind had stopped ever since the kids left, or shut up, or both). Coyote's canoe lay upside down next to the shore, its green thermoplastic hull reflecting sparks of sun. Coyote stepped toward the lake. He made no sound on the carpet of pine needles and moss. He stepped again. Silence. High in the canopy overhead a Canadian jay called. A chickadee whistled. A veery played its slide flute through a long descending scale from the forest upperstory.

Coyote surveyed the campsite. The Little Coyotes hadn't bothered to clean up their stuff, needless to say. Flecks of foil gum wrappers emerged from the mouth of their tent. Jay flew down and gathered up the wrappers. Naughty, naughty, he chided.

Coyote decided he needed to relax a bit before concentrating on a strategy. But first, a Snickers bar.

Coyote chuckled to himself. He always maintained a private stash of Snickers bars in the canoe. Didn't even tell the wife and kids about them. And of course they don't have a scent, with their fiendish new plastic wrappers, so the bears didn't find them.

He rolled over the canoe and removed the Styrofoam flotation block from underneath the bow. Only very sharp eyes could detect the razor line where Coyote cut the block in two and hollowed out the core to fit a six pack of jumbo Snickers bars. He had secured the panel with minimal pieces of Magic Tape that disappeared over the Styrofoam. Perfect. And all done after midnight when the rest of the family was sound asleep.

He sat on a flat rock, now warming in the morning sun, with the Styrofoam flotation panel on his lap. He carefully slit the invisible tape with his claw and opened it up with a squeak.

Damn. A note. In Coyote Woman's fluid paw-writing.

Coyote,

Not my favorite, Snickers bars. I prefer Godiva, or better yet truffles hand rolled by Belgians. But these will do. I knew you had to have some chocolate somewhere. I couldn't help myself. Next thing I knew they were all gone. Have a good trip. And make sure the Little Coyotes brush their teeth. I don't care if you are camping out, vigilant tooth care is essential. In the meantime, I'll be pursuing an interesting opportunity in the islands. As for the rest of your life, take care. Which I know you won't.

Signed,

After Midnight Madness.

PS Next time, don't leave white Styrofoam crumbs all over the floor, please. If there is a next time.

Coyote slowly closed the empty flotation panel. He looked up over the lake into the eye of the sun which was generating enough heat to cause a few ripples of breeze. They appeared in occasional patches on the surface of the lake like clumps of dark scales on the back of the enormous muskellunge that Coyote would fish for later in the day. The pine needles and maple leaves whispered just the faintest music. And the veery again played his flute out of the forest nearby. His stomach rumbled in response. It is going to be a beautiful day, Coyote said.

Coyote lay down on the warm rock at the water's edge and listened to the lake water lapping at the shore. He curled his tail around him, a furball surrounded by sun and soft warm rhythmic lapping. He fell asleep. He dreamed.

He dreamed that he was present at the beginning of the earth. He dreamed that he walked around gingerly among spouting volcanoes and ribbons of bright lava. He dreamed that he held his hand over his head as the rains congealed and fell for millions of years and became oceans. He dreamed that he strolled the margins of these oceans for epochs, stirring his feet in the sand. He saw himself peering into the musty margins of the sea as the earth grew soft and pliable beneath him. He cupped his paws together and scooped up water from the warm margins and saw that it was full of bits and bits of tiny arrangements. As he looked at the water, absorbed in its geometries, a storm came up behind him. Lightning flashed and illuminated the sky. Another lightning bolt struck him and sent a charge through his spine and his fur and his eyes directly into the water he intently held in his hands. And he thought, in the instant before he dropped the warm water back into the sea, he thought he saw the geometries twist themselves together, and duplicate themselves, and move. And the earth turned green and lush around him. And he howled with laughter.

He dreamed that he walked on past the buzzing and scurrying of insects and the trumpeting of reptiles and the flapping of birds. He dreamed that the waters rose and fell and the ice came and went and came and went and cities grew and crumbled and comets passed by. And he was still there, his fur wrapped around him, keeping his laughter warm.

Coyote woke. The sky was black and roiling. Huge gusts of wind and rain were sweeping across the lake toward him. As he sat up, the first gust hit and sent his tent up into the trees to shred and wrap around branches. The second gust launched his fishing pole into the underbrush where the line played out into impossible tangles among the thorns. The waves came up in an instant and wrapped their arms around his canoe and dropped it repeatedly on the rocks.

Coyote stood. The wind and rain howled in the pines around him, and the waves lashing at his feet. His campsite was swept clean of any sign of habitation.

Coyote looked directly into the wind hurtling over the lake. His fur ran with water. But it was still wrapped warmly around him. He opened his mouth and howled. As he laughed, he tasted the sweet rain.

Chapter 7
Coyote On Tour

COYOTE AND THE RES GIRLS should have been the hottest band in America. His flowing multicolored hand-embroidered cape was frankly smashing, as were his pouncing moves on stage with the microphone. His backup band was equally smashing—four reservation women from tribes around the continent dressed in eclectic assemblages of bright feathers, bones, shells, tin can tops, deer toes, woven cotton belts, satin skirts with geometric or flower patterns, and checkerboard shoes. Bass. Drums. Lead. Rhythm. Great Harmonies. They had it all.

Then why were COYOTE AND THE RES GIRLS playing this tacky open air bandshell in a tiny municipal park next to a reedy lake with the sky a tumultuous black and yellow and the humidity 99% and rain virtually certain to follow?

Unfortunately, Coyote couldn't sing worth a damn.

Howl, yes. Yip, certainly. Laugh, all night. But he couldn't carry a tune. When songs began, he'd get so excited he'd riff off into tumultuous yips and barks and howls and wails, and right then customers would seek out the exit signs despite his inspired moves, his flowing cape, his astounding band.

So, bookings had been scarce since he seduced the Res Girls Band with the nuclear fusion of "heartbeat of the earth" drumming and electric bass funk, keyboard frenzy, falsetto wailing, and Coyote style. He fired their mixed-blood imaginations.

But after a series of one-night stands in cheap neighborhood bars and country roadhouses, mumbles and grumbles could be heard inside the band as well as in the audience. This concert was the last chance to pull something together before the Res Girls walked. Therefore, Coyote was extra pleased as he scanned the turnout from behind the band shell's peeling paint. The benches in the park were practically full.

Had he inspected the crowd more closely, he might not have been so enthused. In this town, Summer Concerts in the Park were free, a gift of the local social service agencies who felt an obligation to exercise the institutionalized and keep rampaging teenagers at bay.

Half the audience consisted of vanloads of the Nursing Home Set—rows of white-haired widows, still chatty, still wise, but not exactly mobile. The green park benches were encrusted with tree branch aluminum walkers and acres of supp-hose and shiny wheelchairs full of doubled-over osteoporosis victims. Additional vans dropped off coveys of brain-addled adults—some with constant beatific smiles, others Furious Crippled Geniuses frozen into immobility by their prescience of a horrible future or their sensitivity to a dark and depthless past.

The rest of the audience was a mixed bag.

Assorted physical fitness freaks paused on the benches and sweated rivers in the ferocious humidity. Bicyclists and roller skaters and Vietnam vets in racing grade wheelchairs and—shit —no legs stopped to check out the commotion. Bikers momentarily rested their Harleys in the parking lot to scratch their tattoos.

Sweating families on their way to the monkey bars and swing sets and sandboxes and teeter-totters fatefully paused at the bandshell to see what was up, generally unaware of the horrible future awaiting them as parents of teenagers. "Who do you think is playing, honey? Is it the local Pops Orchestra? Perhaps the high school string quartet? What does that banner say? COYOTE AND THE RES GIRLS? What do you think that could be?"

Slumped on a back bench was a sullen Small Town Newspaper Photographer on assignment with his long lens hanging around his neck like an albatross. Jeez, he thought, what was he doing in this burg, he had Big

City Newspaper dreams, if only he could afford a 28 mm wide angle and a zoom.

Finally, there were The Teenagers, the only volunteers on this musical suicide mission. Burning hot asphalt on their skateboards couldn't have kept them away. They were attracted here, as everywhere else in the world, by the incomprehensible elixir called Rock and Roll.

Coyote knew all about Rock and Roll. How it had originated in medieval Europe as an infectious tune played by the Pied Piper to lure the children to leave their bourgeois parents like bewitched rats leaving a rotting town. Today thousands of Electric Pied Pipers with tattoos were leading yet another generation to their paradises inside crystal mountains with no Moms and Dads to hassle them, no dishes to wash or beds to make or corn to tassel, a terminal euphoria.

Coyote knew the kids would do anything, including getting up before dawn and waiting in line in freezing weather for their tickets with a month's worth of scavenged lunch money in their hands. They'd even work. They worked to support their Rock and Roll habit while fences remained unpainted, dishes unwashed, rooms uncleaned, beds unmade, homework undone, wastebaskets unemptied, cigarettes and dope stashed in old shoes, candles and old wax melted around, walls spray-painted with Basic Truths and scrawled with phone numbers.

Teenagers were perpetually on the prowl for the newest Pied Piper of Rock and Roll, and who knows, COYOTE

AND THE RES GIRLS could be it.

If only Coyote could sing.

As the Res Girls took the stage, lightning flashed out over the lake and the sky rumbled. Uh oh. Parents of the swing set began to pack up their diaper bags. The elderly women draped their blue hairdos with plastic shawls, while their van drivers headed to warm up the vans. The heavenly exit signs were flashing red.

But before the rumbles of thunder scared anyone too far off, the Res Girls set up a terrific backbeat. Drums boomed. Cymbals crashed. The bass throbbed. Magnified through the massive matching speakers,10,000 gigawatts of amplified power, the heavenly thunder struck the audience like an extra heartbeat. The whine of the electric piano mimicked the whine of the sunset mosquitoes rising up from the swampy lake. The lead guitarist started riffing at the moment the wind whooshed up out of the clouds and pulled at the torn T-shirts and French braids of the teenagers, the tattoos of the bikers, the kerchiefs of sweating joggers, the plastic shawls of aged widows, the slack smiles of etherealized adults. The wind awakened the leaves of the park's oaks and the needles of pines like a powerful moan of asthmatic breathing, suffusing the whole region with a supernatural power.

Just then the Res Girls hit the microphones with their high-pitched falsetto wailings, their deep rhythmic harmonies, their doo-wop doo-wop syncopations, their coordinated shimmering movements, their deep spiritual understanding.

And Coyote pounced onto stage, his cape of many colors flying in the wind. He pawed. He whirled. He danced. He grabbed the microphone stand and dramatically thrust it side to side. Then he leaned forward toward the audience and closed his eyes and opened his mouth to sing.

Lightning struck. Right on the bandshell. An electric fire ran up and over the peeling arc, casting a fiery halo over the entire band. The *thump thump thump* of the drums and the electric bass fell in perfect sync with the thunder booms and lightning-strobed whitecaps kicked up on the lake by the sudden wind.

"Aieee…" Coyote wailed into the microphone, into the teeth of the storm, into the stunned crowd of elders, paraplegics, psychotics, schizophrenics, joggers, bikers, vets, teenagers, and parents running for cover with their children.

Storm made Coyote sound good. Very good. Even as oak leaves and pine needles blew across his tongue.

The Bent-overs straightened and boogied on the benches with their aluminum walkers stabbing the sky. The stainless-steel wheelchairs spun in elegant do-si-dos. Supp-hose pumped blood. Psychotics cracked ice. Smilers smiled. Joggers cooled. Bikers roared. Toddlers whipped 360s on the monkey bars. The vets declared victory. The parents relaxed.

Only the teenagers sat wide-eyed and stone still. Their Small-Town Memorial Bandshell had been transformed before their awestruck eyes into the stuff of their most fevered imaginations. It was as if a radiant extraterrestrial disc was hovering low over their very own municipal park. And Coyote was the Prince of the Aliens, speaking directly to their open and unformed souls. What he was saying would someday set them free.

Everybody said it was the most amazing concert they had ever attended. The local newspaper's ninety-two-year-old editor ran his first ever *National Enquirer*-type banner headline. The front-page photograph shot by the suddenly wide-awake photography intern was picked up by the AP and run nationwide. It showed COYOTE AND THE RES GIRLS surrounded by a halo of fire. He would later win the Pulitzer as newspaper photographer of the year.

COYOTE AND THE RES GIRLS were hot. Bookings came in from around the country. Every open-air band shell wanted the act. MTV wanted the video. Record companies faxed contracts for the song.

But Coyote quit. Hung up his cape. Pulled his electric plug.

Rock and Roll was driving him deaf. He could no longer hear his old inner music, the ancient beat that had kept him howling for millennia before electricity was bottled, not to mention wired. Unamplified music, not gigawatt power, made him who he was, the funkiest natural singer ever to laugh at the silence of the moon. He needed to stick with what he knew.

So while the Res Girls signed autographs until their fingernail polish wore out, Coyote drove away from a scheme that worked. This one wasn't worth it.

Without their front man, the Res Girls held hasty auditions. A shy lady named Rose strolled in from an urban street corner reservation where she had been selling beadwork and bagging groceries and singing around the summer powwow circuit. A fox she was. With a voice like an archangel in heat.

ROSE AND THE RES GIRLS went on to smash appearances at St. Paul's Riverfest, Milwaukee's Summerfest, Chicago's Lake Front Fest, Atlanta's Red Mountain Fest, New York's Central Park Fest, and the Hollywood Bowl. The truth had been discovered. They were elemental. They were hip. They were powerful. And without Coyote, they were damn good. They were also making a bundle.

Coyote Woman saw the front-page picture in the *L.A. Times* entertainment section the day she returned from the Pacific, seasick and bored out of her skull. "Damn that Coyote," she said, "he's onto something this time." She immediately called the band to book them for a big concert event she had dreamed up when she was not hanging over the rail. It would take place on the summer solstice. In the Black Hills. It would celebrate the heartbeat of North America.

She asked to talk to the lead singer. She was put through to Rose. Surprised to find the voice wasn't Coyote's,

Coyote Woman knew at the first touch of that fragrant aural vessel that Rose was a winner. She booked the band immediately. And by the way, she asked, what happened to Coyote? Nobody knew, said Rose. On the road again, the Res Girls said, somewhere in the Thunderbird. Oh well, Coyote Woman said to herself, I'll find him when I need him. I always do.

At that moment, Coyote and Thunderbird were cruising rural back roads looking for a place to eat, the wind blowing through his whiskers the way he liked it. He absentmindedly flipped on the radio. The DJ came on, "... and now here's Rose and the Res Girls in the Number One Hit on the fusion charts: 'Give Me Liberty and Make Me Deaf.'" It was his song.

Coyote changed the station. "...that deaf, dumb, and blind kid / sure plays a meeean pinbaaall...." He turned the radio off.

Coyote parked the Thunderbird next to a marsh nestled between sand hills and let the wind ripple slowly through the rushes and into the quiet of his fur. Frogs croaked and whistled back and forth across the reeds, calling for lovers. He tilted his throat to the moon and celebrated their musical gift.

Chapter 8
Coyote Plays Ball

The World Series. Last Game. The Indians were playing the Rangers in Cleveland in the open-air stadium, one of the last open-air stadiums in North America. Only a few thousand acres of asphalt parking lot and freeway and beach and oil sludge and beer cans and plastic bags separated the stadium from beautiful Lake Erie, shimmering turquoise with silent PCBs and PBBs and heavy metals lingering like morays in the finely ribbed bottom sands.

Coyote was sitting in the left field stands guzzling hot dogs with sauerkraut, popcorn, fresh roasted peanuts, ice cold pop, and steaming hot coffee. He was whooping and cheering for the Indians, scoffing and debasing the Rangers, stomping up and down, belching and farting, the stadium rocking and thundering with his enthusiasm under high blue cirrus-stratus clouds with a clear gentle breeze blowing in off the lake.

Seventh inning stretch, the Indians leading two-to-one, Coyote stood up and aired out a mighty belch of fiery onions and sauerkraut and mustard and coffee, the breeze wafting Coyote odors and detritus and bad manners over the entire stadium. “That’s it, the last straw. Throw him out,” said The Management in serious discussion with the League Brass.

“Hey, you can’t do that,” said Coyote. “This is my team. I’m an Indians fan to the end. Not to mention I can’t stand the Rangers. Not to mention I’ve taken off work for the whole season just to be here. Indians going to WIN this time!” said Coyote, the hometown crowd shouting “Yeah, yeah!” and rising to his defense.

Nevertheless, Coyote found himself forcibly bounced outside a high, thick cyclone fence, a gate spiked with barbed wire crashing behind him, *SLAM*. Big, tough toothless uniformed guys smiled at him through the fence, him standing there with his Indians hat on sideways, yellow mustard droplets festooning his whiskers, giant coffee cup in his paw, popcorn box under his arm, ketchup spotted down his breast like fresh war wounds, pink gum wads dotting his sneakers. A serious ball fan. He looked good.

But let me tell you about his hat. A genuine Cleveland Indians baseball hat, transformed by Coyote into a power symbol of the Trickster profession. The edge of the bill was beaded with bright colored beads in geometric patterns, the circular Indians patch on the front likewise brightly beaded into Woodland runes. The adjustable plastic back strap was hung with strips of ermine and beaded clumps of Flicker feathers and sage. Hanging down further on bright yellow and orange strands of electrical wire were two bottle openers with beaded handles. They made music together in the breeze.

The hat was enough to send those remotely knowledgeable about the true powers of the American continent scurrying for cover, whether or not they had ever heard of Coyote and his antic tricks. But the Security goons just stood there looking so mean, ignorant as stones.

As they stared through the fence at each other, Coyote and the guards heard the crowd roar, stand up and roar "Oh no," *stomp, stomp, stomp*, "he hit one out," *stomp*, "he hit one out. Honus the Mighty Ranger! Hit one out. There it goes. Oh no, the Rangers will tie it up, probably win. Oh no, it can't be, not again!" as the ball cleared the upper deck and the outside fence and landed right in Coyote's open coffee cup. *SPLASH.*

"Damn," he said, licking warm droplets off his whiskers with his tongue. He quickly grabbed the ball and threw it back over the fence, high over the upper deck, down over the lower deck, back into the infield, into the fat round mitt of the Indians' catcher, who made the tag at the plate. "They got him at home, they got him!" the crowd stomped, popping rivets throughout the upper deck superstructure, setting off harmonic vibrations converging with fundamental geologic faults, recording seismic bumps and grinds as far away as Trenton, St. Louis, and Mobile. Eyes on the frothing, frustrated, fiery fans, the umpires previewed instant nightmares of their early and unpleasant demise. "He's out!" said the umps. "Wait a minute, the tag doesn't count, it can't count. The ball was on its way to Lake Erie!" protested the Rangers. "He's out!" stomped the crowd.

Coyote picked up his popcorn and his coffee cup and strolled through the parking lot over to the waiting Thunderbird, got in, *ouch, ouch*, damn, left the top down, the black seat roasted in the hot sun. The red Thunderbird had been waiting in the parking lot all day, broiling the black genuine Naugahyde upholstery while burning the tires on acres of hot asphalt. "Let's go," said Coyote, sitting on his cool tail, putting his foot to the floor, pedal to the metal, claws to the curb as the Thunderbird snaked out through ten thousand parked Toyotas and Chevys under the shadow of the Sohio Oil office tower and churned out over the beaches of Lake Erie, beautiful blue-green Lake Erie, shallow, explosive but yes and there are hopeful fish in it again Lake Erie, cruising now over the turquoise water with twisting waterspouts churning up from his wake, big white angry accidental whispering waterspouts one from each drive wheel, waterspouts rising up off the lake heading right for the stadium, right for the Texas Ranger dugout, behind two-to-one at the top of the ninth but with the bases loaded, only one out, oh no, the Indians can't lose again, cannot afford to lose again! On came the waterspouts, the crowd rising up to its feet, stomping, watching, urging on the huge water twisters careening in off the lakefront, hovering into the stadium, catching the Rangers and League Brass off guard, flooding the infield to a depth of six feet, calling the game.

The Indians won! The Indians won! It's about time, thundered the crowd.

Coyote and Thunderbird shuffled off to Buffalo, wet with the spray of freshwater waves. In the rearview mirror, Coyote watched the waterspouts secure the win and yipped his excitement. He thought about the real World Series, the Mother Earth Series. Can't wait, he thought. He could taste sensational plays yet to be made, the future of life as we know it on the line.

What he couldn't see was Coyote Woman watching the game of the week on her big-screen TV at her new concert promotion office in Keystone, South Dakota. But she certainly saw him. "Nice catch, Coyote," she said, and set out after him. She'd forgotten what a powerful player he could be.

Chapter 9
Coyote Saves White Buffalo Woman

All the waitresses in the legendary Buffalo Woman Cafe in Buffalo had black, shiny well-brushed hair with hand-beaded hairclips, except Adora, the owner, who had brown stiff hair, as she was wearing a wig over her white mane. Her wig was not a vanity but served as a convenient hat that saved enormously on time in the morning, time otherwise spent fixing up hair, heck she'd rather be fixing soup, which she did day in and day out, six days a week, part of the breakfast-lunch restaurant service biz. "Heck no, I don't do dinners," said Adora, "I serve only the breakfast boys, the lunch boys. My Boys. They should go home for dinner."

The waitresses and grill cooks, all Natives, had all been there for years. They hustled around the tables flapping jacks like bats with radar. They were from Canadian/U.S. border country and pledged allegiance to neither flag and went back and forth across the border like both countries were home. They made this place hum. Only the dishwasher guy was new. "Can't keep a dishwasher for more than a few months," said Adora. "Nobody likes to wash dishes. Now I got me this big guy, long nose, fuzzy tail, real quick when he wants to be, although he dozes off some too standing in the steam."

Coyote discovered Paradise, he told himself. He loved the homemade soups served with fresh frybread and butter and honey. And the flapjacks, with real maple syrup. And the caramel rolls, big as a wolf's paw. And the motherly service! And the quick jokes, subtle and smooth. This place is heaven.

Coyote failed to mention to himself that he was also broke, i.e. had no money, i.e. empty pocket blues. Dishwashing for soup and frybread and caramel rolls seemed a fair barter. He was stocking up, all he could eat. Hot corn and pepper soup for lunch today. Wouldn't miss it.

But there was trouble brewing along with the coffee at the Buffalo Woman Cafe this morning. Adora had heard the termination rumors. When she grabbed the morning mail and saw the certified letter from the Landlord, she sensed the worst. With Bonnie and Maria and Teresa and Doris and Leslie and Coyote the dishwasher all looking over her shoulder, she opened the letter. Yes, this was it, The Official Termination of the Lease. The Landlord was nobody's fool. "I'm gonna make this old warehouse into a hot spot, Adora.

Rehabilitation. I'm no scumbag. I'm making this a better place. People will pay a lot more for hairdressing and window dressing than they will for salad dressing, ha ha, get it? No way the Buffalo Woman Cafe can make it here any longer. So what all your food is homemade, chopped, sliced, diced, bashed, and burned right there, I'm quadrupling the rent. Hell, Adora, I've let you stay here a generation with no rent increases to speak of, went down, in fact, in constant dollars, but now I finally see Big Possibilities in Warehouse District rehab. I've hung on. Now I'm going for it. Start another restaurant, Adora, you deserve it. Somewhere else. In thirty days or less."

"Ouch," flinched Adora. "Ooooo," moaned the Loyal Long-Term Staff. "Aieee," wailed Coyote. "Well, back to work," said Adora. "My Boys is on their way, and we have thirty more days to serve. We'll think of something."

Six AM outside the Buffalo Woman Cafe the trucks were beginning to pull up—UPS drivers, postal drivers, delivery drivers, food truck drivers, van drivers, pickup drivers. They were all ready for a morning fix of endurance derived from Buffalo Woman's magic brew of caffeine, sugar, butter, honey, maple syrup, and motherly attitude: "The pot is always on Boys, the fry bread and caramel rolls are always fresh Boys." The Boys didn't know about the termination letter stuffed down the front of Adora's housedress between her two huge road map, childless breasts. The place was doomed.

"This is a sad situation," said Coyote. "Here's what I'm going to do. Wait a minute. I don't know what I'm going to do. I'm just going to do it. Here goes."

Coyote pulled on his beaded Indians power hat and began to dance. He danced out from behind the stainless-steel double bin sink and out from behind the counter. He was revving up his inner pounce music. He was beginning to make a spectacle of himself.

Adora, for one, was relieved that he was at least dancing alone, because Coyote was nothing if not a crummy dancer with others. She had learned that months ago when Coyote had swept in with his red Thunderbird and power cap and asked for a job at the legendary Buffalo Woman Cafe and began a demonstration of sweeping up the floor with his tail. "A good trick, but hold down the dust," she said. So he inhaled deeply and sucked in the dust and blew it out the back door where he accidentally sandblasted several parked pickup trucks but the place was clean. "A good trick," said Adora. Coyote was on a roll and started to dance. He grabbed Adora by her housedress and whirled her around and around, which encouraged much whooping by the early AM patrons (who did not know about their etched pickups) and Adora thought it kind of fun too for about thirty seconds or so but then his constant stomping on her feet and his unreadable leading and his tickling furry countenance and let's face it his Coyote early-morning breath reminded her that she had forty eggs and flapjacks on the grill, and although Doris the Onondaga from Upstate was in charge of the grill and hadn't burned anything in seventeen years, nevertheless Adora felt a sudden need to have a supervisory look.

In fact, she went back to her soup, which sat in piles of shredded this and chopped that and handfuls of herbs and hot peppers next to a big old carbon steel chopping knife and two huge aluminum pots with industrial handles and in went all the stuff for it was already 7 AM and the soup's gotta be ready by eleven for the noon Boys. "By the way, Fur Dancer, you're hired," said Adora.

Today Coyote's dance solo took him pouncing out the front screen door, careful not to slam it behind him, and into the street. There he twisted and writhed and stomped into a trance to the beat of the hidden rhythms under the asphalt. The dance proved ineffective, although many who saw it said he had a funky rhythm with his beaded beer openers and ermine tails swinging off his hat.

He attracted attention when he ended up dancing blindly out into the westbound lanes of the nearby freeway. Cars stopped and honked. "Get out of the highway, you asshole! I've got to get to work. My wife, my husband, my kids, my life depend on it!" Coyote danced on, but nothing much positive was happening, so he stopped and ambled back across the freeway toward the cafe, pissing off more drivers.

He decided to run around the building. As fast as he could. Which was fast. Why not? So he ran around it and around it and around it. This had an effect. He created a whirlwind. The whirlwind tore the building off the foundations and floated it up into the sky with Coyote still running around it—into the thick carbon monoxide and nitrous oxide and sulfur dioxide blanket over greater downtown Buffalo with all its snow and rain and industrial lakefront and the Buffalo Bills. "Wait a minute, there's the Buffalo Bills' stadium. Look, there's a game on!" thought Coyote, distracted as they flew over. "How they doing? The Buffalos losing again? Hey, nice pass."

So the restaurant came down with a crunch in the middle of the sidelines of Buffalo Bills' stadium just behind the fifty-yard line. Some of the caramel rolls tipped on their plates and some of the coffee cups nearly spilled and some of the flapjacks flipped themselves.

Adora and her crew accepted the surprise transfer. They took over the concessions franchise at the Bills stadium. More fans than ever attended the games. They loved the fry bread, the caramel rolls, the soup, the coffee.

And Coyote loved the ball games. He was for the Buffalos, back from the brink of extinction, every time. One cold playoff game with the thieving 49ers, he came out from making coffee and washing dishes under the stadium to yell and cheer and stomp and relax in the snowfall. He got thrown out for pouring soapsuds and coffee grounds on the referees. OK. OK. He and Thunderbird shuffled off from Buffalo.

But not before Coyote Woman, watching the playoffs, got another TV fix on his antic smile. She lit out for Buffalo but missed him by a hair.

Chapter 10
Coyote Moves to the City

Coyote and the Thunderbird sat rumbling and smoking and belching and snarling and wheezing and frustrated. They were sandwiched between Toyotas on either side, a Beamer in front all spiffy and pricey, a rusted Chevrolet beater behind, all surrounded by an armada of buses.

No wind in his whiskers, as Coyote liked it. No gravel spewing from beneath the rear wheels, as he liked it. Only Gridlock. How could this have happened?

In Coyote's normal driving story, gridlock was unknown. Coyote and Thunderbird would turn miles out of the way, discover sneaky routes up gravel roads, scrabble over mountains, through parks, around lakes, screech around the corners of sleeping neighborhoods, cut across vacant baseball diamonds, howl past grocery stores already open with people out polishing apples, thread through narrow alleys behind liquor stores, laundromats, and breakfast cafes dripping blobs of grease down the walls beneath the exhaust fans. Coyote always avoided traffic jams. It was his gift.

But today Coyote was in a big one. Perhaps he had made a mistake after all in moving to the city. For millennia he had been a backcountry desert and mountain and prairie kind of guy. He'd hang out with the horned toads and the skunks and the badgers and have a high old time. When the first humans came, he got along fine with them as well. He'd sit on the edges of their villages. He'd talk with their dogs. He'd sneak some food. He'd steal fire for them and from then at considerable risk to himself. He'd teach the people how to laugh. That was his job and he was happy to do it.

But in the last several hundred years, new people came—pale as ghosts, drinkers of spirits, and jumpy as hell. They didn't know how to laugh, and they wouldn't learn. They shot at him constantly. Trapped him. Fenced him. Poisoned him. Strafed him from airplanes. Bombed him. Yet they were so dumb. They kept placing herds of tasty sheep right in front of him. He was very fond of sheep. Sheep are so dumb.

But with all the shooting and the poison on his home range, he had to spread out. Get out of their way. Go where they weren't. But after a while, they were nearly everywhere. So Coyote decided instead, why not go where they were thick as thieves. They'd never notice him. He'd blend right in.

The suburbs proved surprisingly compatible. Coyote developed a considerable fondness for house cats and small domestic dogs. Some wags credit him with the beneficial eradication of that nastiest of human sycophants, the yapping Chihuahua. He loved the gardens too. Especially melons and berries. Garbage cans weren't all bad either. Look, these people throw away practically everything!

So Coyote reasoned that if living in the suburbs was fat city, living in the thick of the city should be paradise. Unfortunately, he picked a bad day to make his move.

The season was hot summer. Already at 7 AM the sky was a burning blue. Since dawn Coyote's driving route had been secretly mined by trucks trailing egg cases of fluorescent orange cones. All possible exits were spiked with backhoes, jackhammers, dump trucks spewing gravel, pickup trucks full of picks and shovels, front end loaders bouncing back and forth across one lane or the other, and stone-faced supervisors standing strategically here and there.

At the end of it all, a huge fat green praying mantis machine sat munching up old asphalt. It sat in the center of the one single thoroughfare essential to every commuter in this part of the city. It chewed and belched, chewed and belched.

The Highway Department Devils had done their work well. Tens of thousands of vehicles, all nearly as practiced and sneaky as Coyote in eccentric commute solutions, were caught by surprise.

Pearl Harbor. Bodies were everywhere. The most damaged were those who listened too long to the early AM disc jockeys, a species so infected with irresponsible madness as to drive even Coyote over the parking ramp wall. But even honest news junkies overdosed on the reruns of Morning Edition from National Public Radio, the erudite voices and commentaries driving them mad with responsibility and concern.

Coyote at least switched off his radio. That was easy. But he was still trapped. Acres of poisonous air drifted up around him. Coyote could sense somewhere ahead the vanishing point of orange cones as they finally succeeded in urging six lanes of traffic into five, then four, then three, then two, then one.

Then none. Thousands of vehicles seemed to vanish through the squeeze barrier, their molecules vaporized—cars, trucks, buses, delivery vans, all finally pushed through the eye of the needle to The Other Side. To Bizarroland. China. Time warp. Anti-matter. Space debris. Quiet snow-capped Tibetan mountaintop, car bodies rusting coolly in sunlit snow.

Coyote wasn't ready for vaporization. Not yet. Not him. He couldn't disappear yet. He hadn't completed his task on this continent, whatever it was. He looked around desperately. The Thunderbird groaned and snarled in near terminal frustration. Which way was OUT?

The answer, Coyote finally deduced, was surprisingly simple. Can't go forward—there's a dying Beamer. Can't go left—there's a boiling Toyota. Can't go right—there's another boiling Toyota. Can't back up—there's a dead Chevy beater with a greasy longhaired guy ransacking hoses underneath the hood. Around them all were buses thick with fetid commuters.

Can't go down—there's rotten, frost-heaved asphalt, it's worn yellow lines guiding thousands of crazed commuters to their doom.

There is only up.

Coyote turned off the ignition and leaned back. The Thunderbird shuddered a powerful sigh and fell silent. Coyote drew a deep breath of vile air. He blew it high over the camera shops and pharmacies and luggage stores and high-rise offices around him.

He put his hands behind his head and took a long look at the slit of high blue morning sky between the high-rise canyon walls above him. He saw, or thought he saw, a wisp of high cirrus cloud. Was it a horse's tail? Or a bunny's tail? Or a coyote's tale? Hard to tell.

But it was not hard to close his eyes. It was not hard to tell himself a cool story. He made it up as he went along.

Here's the cool story he told.

Coyote was on the shore of a huge mountain lake. He stood on the shore, his back shaded by the black oriental shadows of ponderosa pines clutching rocks. He looked deep into the crystalline water. Down ten feet, down twenty feet, he saw himself sitting, cool as a bottom stone, quiet water floating his fur around him. Coyote sat under the cold clear water with the sunlight radiating down in front of him in slow white shafts. Only the silver bubbles of his scuba breathing broke the silence. As he sat there, cool and still, an image of impossible loveliness scuba-dived toward him. She was naked except for a multicolored buoyancy vest, blue mask, snorkel and fins, and a gleaming stainless-steel eighty cubic foot compressed air tank. The fine human hairs of her arms and legs each trapped a silver bubble of air, clothing her in diamonds. Her lips caressed the regulator, enfolding it. Those lips—destined to return the art of kissing to the silver screen. Yes. Yes! It was Mavis Clovis, the girl of his dreams. She nearly touched him as she glided past, his fur fluttering in the soft current of her expert strokes. He turned and followed her rising bubbles into the liquid of the heart.

Chapter 11
Coyote Falls in Love

"Coyote Does Windows." That was the advertisement plastered up on telephone poles, trees, and kiosks around the city. Plus the local phone number: 212-269-6837. And the phone was ringing off the hook. Business was hot.

Apparently, no urbanites wanted to do windows anymore. Oddly, the status of window washer in the land of glass mountain ranges was beneath contempt. Were urban gangs too busy banging to clean up? Or were urban humans simply too busy looking inward or downward to notice the grime-frosted glass around them?

Coyote didn't know. All he knew was that he needed something called a job.

This moving to the city wasn't all bread and roses, he'd found. Parking was impossible, for one. And expensive for another. You want to keep a car, you gotta pay. Nothing in his immortal birth certificate said he had a right to keep anything but the fur on his back. And Coyote wanted to keep this car. He and Thunderbird had come a long way together.

So Coyote looked around for a work opportunity. He began by looking through his own subsidized apartment window, which was impossible due to the layers of urban grime greasing the outside. All he could see was his own reflection. No wonder no one has any perspective anymore, thought Coyote.

So he schemed up the window-washing business.

His first job, he was to clean a small rehabilitated warehouse office building on Second Avenue.

Actually, "office building" pushed the concept considerably. In fact it was a converted warehouse with loft space for artists, writers, advertising maniacs, illustrators, typesetters, and other low overhead entrepreneurs. In other words, it was cheap.

The rehab had been confined to a new front door and new anodized aluminum frame windows on the first floor and the placement of a large green striped awning over the door as a sign of progressive taste and new leadership. Above the first floor, no change. The owners were cheap. They smelled of martinis and open shirts with gold chains and overextended mortgages and Mercedes dreams.

Coyote was cheap too. It was a perfect match. He got the contract, payment upon completion.

Coyote arrived at the site at the crack of dawn and parked the Thunderbird in a "No Parking Zone—U.S. Mail." He planned to finish a floor of windows and be out of there before the first mail pickup at eight AM.

He pulled his professional window-washing equipment out of the passenger seat of the Thunderbird. He had two large lard buckets rescued from a restaurant trash container. A squeegee borrowed from a self-service gas station. Plus some lengths of rope liberated from unattended boats down at the docks. His washing compound was a tiny vial of blue food dye, a few drops of which when added to water made it look like Windex. That and a bunch of rags were all he needed.

Rags were the hardest to come by these days. He had to beat the bag ladies and bag men to them, and they wouldn't share, not one rag, no sir, these are My Home! He had managed to snare a few, but only with a struggle.

He surveyed the job. The second-story windows reflected the sunrise like bricks. They were magnificent indicators of urban geologic time, encrusted with decades of blown horse manure, dust bowl dust, cheap restaurant grease, and toxic auto and bus and jet exhaust. One window on the back alley had been roped off years ago by a team of student archaeologists writing a dissertation on the evolution of urban society, but their grant ran out and they never came back.

He climbed through the dark hallway and up the metal fire stairs, went into the men's room and filled a bucket, then knocked on the door of the first office, MC Enterprises. "Windows," he announced, and unlocked the door with his fresh master key.

Nobody there. Only an answering machine with a blinking message light, a typewriter, a desk full of yellow Post-it notes, a Macintosh computer and peripherals, some funky Harry Fonseca prints on the brick walls, bookshelves cluttered with books, and sanded and varnished wooden floors strewn with bright Navajo rugs. Comfortable, thought Coyote.

He walked over to the window, pushed it open and climbed out, dragging his water and mop and squeegee and rope with him. He closed the window behind him.

He found himself balancing on a narrow cornice of the old building, just above the new awning declaring the building trendy and ready for a rent increase. The cornice consisted of heavy limestone blocks set into the brick face with mortar that had crumbled to dust decades ago, leaving friction the remaining structural element. Teetering on the cornice, Coyote began to scrub.

As he slowly worked through layer after layer of urban history, he began to be able to see back into the office. He noticed through the opacity that someone was now sitting at the desk. Rubbing further, he saw that it was a woman. She was typing something earnestly into her Mac. As she looked intently at the screen, Coyote saw her face as it washed in the phosphorescent glow. Something about the intensity of her concentration reminded Coyote of someone.

Watching her eager writing, plus the rhythmic circular rubbing on the panes of glass—around, around, around, around—slowly suffused Coyote into a daydream.

He was on a riverbank, with a quiet breeze rustling the silver leaves of the cottonwoods. The leaves flashed their undersides like shook foil in the sun. He was sitting in thick summer grass, warm and pliant in the rhythmic reverie of a story. He had sneaked away from the Coyote family lair and was telling stories, some old ones, some made up as he went along. Like Scheherazade, he was storying as if his life depended on it. And it did.

For reclining in the grass across from him, resplendent in her attention to the mesmerizing drama of his flowing syllables, was Mavis Clovis. She was eighteen, a high school drama star, a dreamer of great dreams, a deep dweller in the fictive process. And a bombshell of nuclear proportions. Coyote was held so rapt in the texture of her gaze that the stories came to him as they never had before, spinning out of his mouth fully fleshed with personal idiosyncrasies and antic betrayals, plotted with foolish attempts and successful surprises, sandwiched with dreams within stories and stories within dreams, one inside the other, stepping down, down, down into the core of life and laughter at the center of the earth. She leaned closer to catch his drift, then closer, then closer into the protective embrace of

Coyote's enfolding fabrications. As she swooned into a vertigo of ecstatic aural entrapment, she wiped a glistening dewdrop of perspiration from her upper lip with the back of her wrist. Her wristwatch glowed before her eyes. Oops, rehearsal time! Gotta go, Coyote. See you soon, I hope.

Coyote's daydream faded as his rubbing on the pane of glass brought it finally to its old crystal clarity and his eyes focused clearly for the first time on the woman at the keyboard. She was perspiring gentle drops like silver beads on the delicate crest of her upper lip. She licked her lips, one and then the other, without breaking her concentration. Those lips.

She pulled the keyboard off her desk and rested it on her lap, typing and typing, her fingers stroking the keys with expert swiftness, the subtle vibrations of the keyboard rippling the folds of her loose dress, ever so slightly jiggling the muscles of her thighs as she wrote. Her fingers moved faster and faster in her lap, the screen bathing her in a halo of phosphorescent pixels, faster and faster, those lips moving closer and closer to the screen, nearly touching it, until in one last stretch of creative completion, she thrust back in her swivel chair, her wet lips glistening, her eyes tightly closed, her fingers wildly flying.

Then she relaxed. A drop of silver dew rolled down her upper lip and off the corner of her mouth. Coyote watched, his eyes bulging into the clear glass. He was as tense as a wire. He knew her. He knew her! Those lips! That ecstatic attention the story! No one did that. No one, that is, but Mavis Clovis. The girl of his dreams.

At which point she opened her eyes. She was still leaning back in her chair, exhausted, for the first time her eyes off the computer screen. For the first time she noticed something aside from her story. For the first time she stared at the surprising hole in the window, illuminated by sunrise. For the first time she saw the outline of Coyote.

She stood up, eyes wide. Her lips formed rich quizzical syllables—"Coy-o-tee?" At which silent syllables the cornice gave way.

Coyote rode the carefully chiseled block of limestone, with its millions of skeletons of ancient sea creatures, down like an elevator. Down through the new striped green awning, down in front of the new glass door, down to shatter the limestone skeletons all over the sidewalk, and to crack Coyote's skull right through his hat.

He woke up days later, white bandages spiraled around his split and splitting head, surrounded by white blankets, white walls, white curtains, and a brown television set mounted on the wall in front of him. It was turned on. Saturday morning cartoons. Wily E. Coyote was chasing Roadrunner down the highway. *Beep, Beep. Varoooooommmmm!*

"Damn," said Coyote, sitting up, "my favorite show. Oooooo!" His head throbbed.

He glanced painfully toward a chair in the corner of his room. Someone was wrapped in a blanket, asleep. Certain roundnesses and fullnesses under the blanket suggested that it was a female with whom he was deeply familiar. The blanket stirred—"Umhmmm, aaahhh"—as the body rolled in the chair. Coyote's eyes ached as he watched the satin edge of the blanket slip down from her face. One long-lashed eye fluttered open and sized him up, and winked. Coyote Woman had finally tracked him down.

Chapter 12
Coyote Bags One

Coyote stepped out for Chinese while Coyote Woman camped on the phone in their apartment, the temporary urban office of Coyote Woman Productions. She was closing deals for her big Black Hills Summer Solstice Concert and was happy to have him temporarily out from underfoot.

Coyote cruised along the city streets, nose in the air, sniffing the rainbow of ethnic food scents, feeling good. He also stumbled off curbs, *ooofff,* crashed into litter barrels, *whump*, walked into "Walk/Don't Walk" poles, *whang*, into construction barriers, *ouch*, into manholes, *stubb*, into other pedestrians, "Excuse me, excuse me," into street vendors, "Watch it, buddy." Clearly Coyote wasn't watching it.

Then something in a funky retail display window captured his attention.

Not the merchandise inside the glass—the plastic manikins in impossible postures draped with the latest designer summer beachwear. No, it was in the glass itself.

The smoky reflections in the window glass made urban street life seem much more… mysterious and exciting and beautiful than if he simply looked around him at the harried people and fuming traffic and immovable objects. In the window reflection colors were richer, faces smoother, bodies softer. Blemishes disappeared. Everyone looked glamorous, mysterious, sexy. Including himself.

Coyote admired for a moment—well, possibly more than a moment—his own presentation in the glass, deeply mirrored against a backdrop of manikins riding windsurfers draped with bright towels. His yellow eyes flickered and shone. His long snout never looked quite so, well, dramatic. His whiskers, brushed back, took on the sweep and curvature of the latest in Swiss windsurfer sails. His twin protruding incisors shone like old ivory. His hair, casually blown back by the urban wind tunnel breeze, looked raffish, aggressively natural.

In short, Coyote looked devastating.

So did everyone else.

He scanned off his own reflection and checked out that of others in the flow of his fellow urban creatures surging along the sidewalk behind him. Just then a gap opened in the river of people and traffic. And he saw her. Across the street. Mavis Clovis, the girl of his dreams!

She stood alone, under the sign of the EVE boutique. Actually not her, but a reflection of her in his windowpane. And she was looking at him!

She was even more rich, more exotic, more beautiful, more romantic than ever before. She shimmered twice golden, fired by a genuine inner mystery as well as beauty.

Her features combined golden highlights with deep cavernous shadows. Her neck echoed the arc of herons, or at least of bitterns, a short *s* curve of barely restrained flight. The exotic cloth sheathing her hair undulated in the wind. Her shoulders flowed with exotic materials from the looms of Central and South America. Her Statue of Liberty form slipped down below the sill of the window and disappeared.

They had eye contact. Or had they? Coyote could not be sure. He stared deeply into her image reflected before him.

One thing he was sure of. When he licked his lips he tasted the pungency of love.

As soon as his cracked brainpan healed after the window-washing accident he had gone out for Chinese and first paid a visit to the office of M. C. Enterprises. But she was long gone. The office was empty. No phone. No forwarding address. No message.

Slowly, so as not to lose her this time, Coyote turned around to gaze directly into her eyes.

No one was there. Only a parking meter, a pathetic urban flower bin, some brief but to the point sidewalk graffiti.

He jerked his head back. A dream? No, back in the window there was her reflection again, powerful as pheromones, under the sign of EVE.

He swiveled again. Across the avenue, again temporarily devoid of traffic if not of fumes, he saw her reflection in the EVE store window in front of a display of fashionable underwear among palm trees and race cars and swimming pools.

Yet she was only half his dream girl now. Still compelling, still tasty, yet the golden highlights were somehow less golden, the deep black shadows somehow less rich, the glint and depth of the eyes somehow less deep, the cut and quality of the scarf a hair less exotic, the curve of the body less statuesque.

Still, Coyote was not fickle. Love is love.

Coyote bounded across the street to embrace the girl of his dreams. He was nearly flattened by a passing billboard disguising a bus. He stopped short, and for agonizing seconds endured before his eyes shocking slogans about tooth decay and the romance that only yogurt can bring while bewindowed heads rolled by impassively.

Finally the bus wheezed by and Coyote darted through the hail of black exhaust, his eyes burning and nose running. He slipped on an oil slick and catapulted into the next lane where a cab nearly struck him. That the cab missed was a terminal disappointment to the driver, for whom the only just compensation was ear-splitting horn honking and a list of imprecations out of some devil's dictionary of the profane, to which Coyote was forced to subject himself due to the fact that he was now wedged between two streams of traffic counterflowing from the poles of Hell.

Coyote's hair was standing on end, a substantial undertaking. Not at the threats of the cab driver, to which Coyote, as well as every other city dweller, was inured. Nor at the traffic jam, which was about as exotic an urban experience as gum on the sidewalk. But because his dream woman was out of sight.

Of course, Coyote is not Coyote for nothing. He bounded out of the bad breath of the cab driver, elegantly farting into his open window as he passed, did a split-second stomp on his roof, and landed, a desperate man, on the sidewalk on the other side.

He looked up the sidewalk. He looked down the sidewalk. She was gone. Nobody there but the hustling urban masses. He looked at the display window of the MADAM I'M ADAM men's shop in front of him. He could not resist again remarking his own dramatic good looks. Then he checked out the EVE boutique next door.

Nobody there but a creature dragging two huge shopping bags. Mavis must have slipped in the door. He dashed in.

Nobody there but a matronly boss slashing price tags. Coyote tore through the dressing rooms. Nobody. Well, nobody but a guy trying on his fifth skirt, and still unable to decide between the chiffon and the plaid for the ball tonight. "Go with the plaid," Coyote suggested as he dashed back onto the street.

Nobody again. Nobody but the fireplug creature with the huge rotting overstuffed bags at her sides staring at the exotic clothing in the EVE shop glass.

Coyote paced past the shop, desperate, desperately confused.

He couldn't resist a final glance at himself in the window, the golden reflection portraying his whiskers in an especially dashing light. And there she was.

He stared wide-eyed at her reflection, her eyes still hooded in mystery, her form scarfed in dreams.

He glanced also, out of the corner of his eye, at the bag lady next to him.

Then back at the reflection, only a single reflection now, not the exotic double reflection from across the street. It was the girl of his dreams. But it certainly was not Mavis Clovis.

Their eyes met in the glass. In the glass they shared an exotic handsomeness. In the glass they both rode out of the Arabian Nights, sat around King Arthur's table, partied in the Kennedy White House, sang and danced at Disney's studio, lived out the American myth of creation.

In the glass their eyes held each other. Important fundamental information was exchanged.

In the glass, Coyote and the mystery bag woman slowly reached out their hands. Their reflections touched, and the touch was the explosion of real touch, of real contact.

Slowly, so as to not disturb the essential connection they had discovered, they glided off together, eyes held fast to the images of each other—and of themselves—in the boutique glass. Love lasted all the way to the limestone pilaster next to the alley. Then it disappeared.

Chapter 13
The Coyote Cab Company

He opened the brand-new Yellow Pages in the phone booth. One ad in the Taxicab section caught his eye:

THE COYOTE CAB COMPANY

Original stories told while you ride.

Toll free: 1-800-COYOTES.

All Thunderbird fleet.

COYOTE: A MYTHOLOGICAL EXPERIENCE

A mythological experience? What could that be? He thought he'd try a trip. He picked up the phone and dialed the toll-free number.

The phone was answered with a flourish of reservation jingle dress clanging and drumming, followed by:

Hello. You have reached Coyote Cabs, the Mythological Cab Company. More than basic transportation, we take you where you need to go. Original stories while you ride. Leave your name and number and Coyote Cabs will get back to you when you're ready to ride. Thanks for calling Coyote Cab. Beeeeep...

A recording. What a tacky way to run a cab company. He was hooked. He left a message: "I'll be right over."

Coyote hung up. He was standing at the pay phone outside his new office. He walked back through the door with the freshly painted "Coyote Cab Company" logo drying on the glass. He settled into his desk chair. He tilted back, put his feet up next to the answering machine and contemplated the first day of business. It felt good. His message was a powerful one.

This idea had to be a bonanza, no matter what Coyote Woman said. Who understood land travel needs better than Coyote? Who detested the texture of the traffic jam, the geometry of gridlock, more than Coyote? Who knew the only two escape routes?

Escape #1: Avoidance. Instead of driving with the traffic, Coyote instinctively turned against it. When everybody was going downtown in the morning, Coyote would take riders out of town. When everyone was going out of town in the evening, he would take them downtown. Who cared what their expected destinations were. Coyote didn't. Coyote cared for their deepest needs.

Escape #2: Stories. This was hardly an innovation. Cabbies have been unloading tales on passengers for generations. Recently, however, the practice had diminished dramatically as few if any cabbies spoke the common tongue. Coyote saw this trend as in his favor. Today's cabbies certainly had many entertaining stories to tell, but nobody but a handful of native countrymen could understand them. Coyote also had many great stories to tell. And he could speak all American languages fluently. It was his gift.

Now if he could only get a customer.

The phone rang. Coyote listened as the recorded message played out. Three quarters of the way through, he heard a voice on the other end growl, "What's this? Screw you, buddy!" Click. *Hummmmm....*

Perfect. That was the last test. His self-selecting mechanism worked. Coyote refused to drive assholes in too big a hurry.

The next caller left her name and phone number. He was in business.

Before he returned the call, he took one last look at his business checklist.

- Yellow Pages Ad. *Check.*
- Office Leased. *Check.* Coyote looked around him. It was a pit. An old warehouse that even the

freelance artists and street people hadn't found yet. Still a warehouse, the bottom floors were jammed with huge boxes of wares. Up the freight elevator it had more potential. Brick walls, wooden floors, huge south-facing industrial windows opaque with grime, enough room for a desk, a chair, an answering machine, a couple of T.C. Cannon posters, a message pad, a Macintosh computer, a Navajo blanket on the floor for a rug (when it got cold, he threw it over his shoulders as a coat), a dusty garage sale couch for naps, and the sign on the wire glass door: COYOTE CAB COMPANY. The office was luxurious by cab company standards. It felt like home.

- COYOTE CAB COMPANY logo designed and approved. *Check.*
- Answering machine message taped. *Check.*
- Radios installed in cabs. Oops, no radios.
- Coyote-type drivers recruited and trained in the Coyote Way. Not yet.
- Numerous cabs leased and outfitted with official Coyote Cab Company logo. Only one, his own '56 Thunderbird parked downstairs surrounded by massive idling diesels.

OK, so here's where the business stood. One cab only, with the logo freshly painted on the doors and the custom neon COYOTE TAXI sign installed over the convertible top so that it would stay there even when the top was down, which was all the time, since the top was broken.

One two-seater cab. No radio. No top. No employees.

OK. He would have to drive the first few calls himself. He called the client back. "This is the dispatcher for the Coyote Cab Company. I'll be right there." He grabbed his hat, recorded a new message for his next inquiries, rode the slow freight elevator to the first floor, jumped into the Thunderbird, squeezed around the diesel trucks and was gone.

He pulled up to the entrance of the fancy midtown hotel in an instant. He jostled for position among his fellow cabbies, who looked with open jealousy at the '56 Thunderbird outfitted with the funky blue and pink neon COYOTE TAXI sign, his convertible top down, his beaded baseball cap and trail of flicker feathers and ermine tails and can openers blowing in the breeze.

On the other hand, they weren't jealous enough to give him an inch versus their own position in line and status in life. Fortunately, his client swiftly emerged from the hotel entrance, saw the flashing COYOTE TAXI neon and waved at him.

She was dressed in a conservative blue Brooks Brothers for Women business suit, with a polka dot upside-down *Y* for a tie, and a brim hat that shaded her face. She was carrying a briefcase big as Coyote's kit bag in which he carried all his trickster supplies until the end of the world. She wore serious horn-rimmed glasses. She had great ankles over Nike running shoes. She had an MBA. And she appeared to be in a hurry.

Coyote pounced out of the cab. He grabbed her briefcase—whew, heavy—and affixed it with bungee cords to the luggage rack over the trunk. He pounced back in. She climbed in. Dust rose from the seat as she sat down.

Make a note, thought Coyote. Beat that seat.

He hit the meter. Wait a minute. No meter. Damn, forgot meters. He patted the dashboard where a meter might have been and glanced in the rearview mirror.

Behind him were ten or twelve muscular cabbies getting out of their cars and converging on his little red Thunderbird with the apparent intention of seeking out his license to operate as a cab company in this or any other city or town or rural area. Coyote pulled down his visor. Damn, no license. Forgot the license. Only the obligatory sign: No smoking, no drinking, no eating, no cussing, no change. Coyote jerked the car out into traffic and quickly disappeared.

"What a shitty meeting," she opined under her breath. "These assholes have zero imagination, and less humor. They wouldn't know a new market opportunity—or a joke—if it drove over them in one of their semis." She looked up, distracted. "Say driver, you never asked me where I wanted to go. I have an appointment on Wall Street. Get me there. But tell me a story on the way. I could use a good story. I knew a guy back in my hometown who used to tell great stories. Get me out of this funk."

"No problem," said Coyote. He began.

Coyote was going along, widening his range, panting like an accordion, tongue drooping like a loose necktie. He was expanding his territory into the tropical jungles, and the humidity was killing him. Coyote didn't like humidity if he could avoid it. So even though the nearby beaches were fecund with turtle nests and the offshore reefs were unspeakably rich and colorful living mountain ranges about which he was intensely curious, he was heading toward the dryer highlands. If he could figure out how to get there.

Pooped, he stopped for directions at a crossroads cantina along the jungle trail. A tin Coca-Cola sign decorated the thatched roof and sides of split bamboo. Coyote noticed several shadowy animal trails radiating into the surrounding wall of dripping green. Although there was a Coca-Cola sign outside, the main drink inside from the scent of things appeared to be local firewater, aguardiente. God, I can't stand that crap, thought Coyote as he stepped into the darkness and up to the bamboo bar. The barkeep was a raving Toucan. His bright-colored schnozz was so huge he was a danger to himself. He knocked bottles off the bar whenever he turned around. To compound the problem, he smoked cigars. One whole side of his beak was stained brown. A nasty habit, thought Coyote to himself. But Toucan was good humored. "Ciao, Señor. Welcome to La Cantina Coca-Cola en la Jongle Publica. *You look tired. OK to rest your tongue on the bar. Everybody else does." He swabbed cigar ashes onto the floor. "How'd you get here, bedraggled one?" asked Toucan. "Just farting around," said Coyote, panting a smile. "Got anything to drink?" "Got aguardiente." "Aiee." Coyote gasped. "OK, OK. for you special, two fresh cervezas." "Beer?" "Beer. Found' em on a dead gringo. Panamanian Red Stripe. That OK? Never opened." "No Coca-Cola?" asked Coyote. "No Coca-Cola," answered Toucan.*

An accomplished scavenger himself, Coyote certainly didn't object to the beer's origin. "OK," said Coyote, dying of thirst, and looked around the room while Toucan popped the cap with his bill.

Next to him at the bar was a monkey with a big mouth. A two-fisted drinker, he extended his tail, "Howler's the name, tree talk's my game." Coyote shook the tail, then looked around at the other tables. At a booth on the side a couple of pit vipers were discussing the relative merits of lying in wait for prey on the ground versus dropping from trees. At a smaller table two bright-red poisonous tree frogs chirped to each other about the merits of various bromeliad condominiums. Coyote surmised by the color of the discussion that one had a couple of hot properties to sell. At the darkest table in the corner a pair of huge yellow eyes stared at him. Yikes!!! A jaguar! Coyote's fur raised up all over his body. "Don't worry," said Howler. "No preying allowed in here. Toucan is strict about that." As they talked, a couple of tapirs strolled in. They sat at a round table and ordered banana splits.

Still thirsty, Coyote ordered the second cerveza. "By the way," Coyote asked Toucan, "what happened to the gringo?" One of the pit vipers spun around with a big smile on his face. "A petroleum engineer," he grinned.

Coyote turned to face the bar crowd. No regular drinker, he was feeling pretty good, cerveza style. "Say you guys," he said. "I'm from up north. A pretty tricky guy. Any of you seen this before?" He took out his eyes and started juggling them. Nobody seemed impressed. He heard only yawns and hisses. So he grabbed the lighted cigar out of Toucan's mouth and juggled that along with the eyes. "Three things. Not bad," croaked one of the frogs. "But we got a Fox guy down here who can juggle both his eyes, plus a cigar, plus his asshole." "Hey, no sweat," said Coyote. So he took out his asshole and juggled all four. Except he got the cigar too close to his asshole in the air and burned it. Ouch, said Coyote. And dropped his eyes. Before he felt around to pick them up, he stooped to put his asshole back. But he put the lit cigar there by mistake, at the same time putting his asshole into Toucan's beak. "Aieee!" Coyote howled. "Hey, you asshole," Toucan clacked.

The crowd broke up. Rolling on the floor, they were. Even the jaguar had tears running down his cold yellow eyes. Howler's hysterical howls could be heard across several banana republics. A fat tapir retrieved Coyote's eyes. Coyote put them back in. "Pretty damn good, Coyote," said Howler. "That performance beats all." Coyote acknowledged the applause as best he could. His burned butt was killing him, and Toucan was scowling at him as well. He had to throw away the cigar.

"Driver," said the passenger, with tears running down her cheeks. "You sure you know where this story is going?" "No idea," said Coyote. She got out her handkerchief and dabbed at her eyes and blew her nose. "Go on," she said.

Too late. By the time she asked, Coyote had driven across the Great Plains and deserts of North America and through the deep jungles of Central America, leaped the Panama Canal and countless muddy rivers and climbed into the dry temperate heights of Columbia and Ecuador, then down again through the coastal jungles to the slim dusty deserts of Chan Chan and along the cold Pacific bluffs to Lima, then took a left turn winding up into the high Andes. Coyote parked the Thunderbird near the main square of Cuzco. Peru.

"Wall Street," he said.

She looked around her. The stone walls running toward her and away from her were massive, dressed boulders whose graceful curves married to the next stone together without mortar. They were the walls of old Inca palaces shining a golden brown in the high Andean sun. On top of the walls, and married to them, were white plastered walls supporting red tiled Spanish colonial roofs. The windows were barred with grids of wrought iron.

Wall Street. Women in fedoras and men in bare feet and burros with burdens and llamas with bells strolled the cobblestones between the walls.

"Well, well," she said, and slowly got out. "How much?" she asked, rubbing her eyes.

Coyote popped out and unbungeed the briefcase —*oof!*—and handed it to her.

"That'll be two bucks for the ride, five bucks for the story on the way, and an extra fifty cents for the bag. Nice bag."

She wrote him a check for ten. "Keep the change," she said. "Although the story kind of wandered a bit. And touch up the ending. If there is an ending."

A check? Crap, he forgot the No Checks sign. He had to take it.

She picked up her bag and slowly walked down Cuzco's Wall Street, running her fingers along the massive smooth stones as she passed.

Coyote watched her go. There was something familiar about that walk. Then he considered the insouciance of her upper lip that said, "OK, so I have an MBA and now I'm in Cuzco instead of in the financial tunnels of New York City, what can I do with this news?"

As she disappeared down the street, the curves of her body became more abstract as the cobblestones and walls merged into a stone stairway climbing down the steep hill toward the jungles of the western Amazon. The curves, even beneath Brooks Brothers for Women, were, well, rich. And he knew he had seen them before.

As it turned out, he had seen them hundreds of times.

He looked down at the check in his hand. Above the address of a Central Park apartment, Number 14 B, was the name Mavis Clovis. The girl of his dreams.

Coyote pounced up so hard he left his shoes behind, then tore off after her down the Wall Street of Cuzco, tail and nails flying. Down the staircase, he found her briefcase, then her shoes, then her blue suit. Then her glasses. But she had disappeared.

She had wandered off the eastern slope of the Andes and into the swaddling cloud blanket of rain forest. Eventually she lived in village after village, wrapped only in dripping vines with toucans overhead and anacondas underneath. She listened to stories about the origin of The People and learned what and how the people ate and drank and smoked and healed. By the time she returned to North America, she had signed up seven jungle tribes as partners and master suppliers of pharmaceuticals, nuts, gum, and stories to MC Enterprises, Inc., specializing in Rainforest Products.

Chapter 14
Coyote Gets the Message

The first thing Coyote did when he reentered the Coyote Cab Company office was drop his briefcase—well, her briefcase—to the floor. His back was killing him. Too much stuff in there. He'd thrown out all the annual financial reports and business plans he'd found in there—how does anyone read those things anyway? But he kept the case with the initials MC on the clasp. In it he put all the fascinating stuff he picked up on the trip home, from Cuzco streets, jungle highways, rural fiestas, and urban garbage cans. He was an aficionado of great stuff.

Bedraggled as he was, Coyote was feeling pretty good. He sported a wild red tie and stained seersucker coat scored at a suburban church basement sale. Secretly, he was getting into flashier dress. Was slightly disappointed he wasn't a bird, where the male of the species stands out in the forest.

His bland desert camouflage no longer seemed to suit him. Is that why he scratched around so much? Was he looking for color? He didn't know. Maybe the answering machine did.

He pushed the message button. But instead of answers, Coyote ran into more questions. People apparently had had some difficulty understanding his last outgoing message.

When he left the office he'd added Anishinabe drum and falsetto flourishes recorded off a 1905 Edison disc, over which he'd dubbed the beginning of a wandering story. Unfortunately, he forgot to mention Coyote Cabs. Damn.

So this morning he heard a series of blank hums and beeps and clicks and curses in response to the vague message. Amazingly, mixed in with the curses were two or three actual orders for cab rides. In addition, a sultry female voice said she was responding to the one-inch column advertisement in the *International Enquirer* promising: *Successful travelling career for theatrically inclined woman who enjoys writing stories and hearing them told. Call 1-800-COYOTES.*

Coyote perked up. On the way back from Peru, passing through Mexico, his heart broken, he dreamed a fresh scheme. He phoned in the ad from a truck stop in Nogales. And here she was already answering his howl.

Upon closer examination, however, Coyote recognized the message as the thinly disguised voice of Coyote Woman. The phone number she left was his own. Damn. He had no idea she read the *Enquirer*.

Then there was the message from *The Sharper Image* catalog indicating that a credit check after his 800 number order from a phone booth in Nogales of the electronic Zen massage chair could not be fulfilled after all due to the apparent cancellation of all his credit card accounts for non-payment of bills, but thanks for calling *The Sharper Image.*

And nothing from Mavis Clovis.

He was about to turn off the tape, pounce on the couch for a nap, then drive a few cab trips, when the decibel level of the tape jumped many orders of magnitude. Coyote was blown onto the floor in a cloud of dust.

"COYOTE!"

My God, it was Dad. Dad, the Guy in the Sky. Dad, who punched the clock of Time and let it go. Dad, who ate volcanoes for breakfast and farted earthquakes. Dad, who watched every spider snare every fly and every mountain lion jump every coyote and every cavalry round up every Indian and every War to End All Wars like they were so many episodes of *Sesame Street.* Dad, who allowed modern cities to become so magnetic that almost everybody lived there or wanted to. Even the destitute. Even Coyote.

"COYOTE! STOP SCREWING AROUND WITH YOUR ANSWERING MACHINE!!!"

The tape went dead. The air crackled with the buzzing of burned phone lines.

Coyote huffed as the dust settled around him. "OK. OK. I get the message," he huffed. "Thanks for the call. I guess."

He got up from the floor and dusted himself off. He picked up the microphone and set the machine on RECORD. He tried for a long time to think of a new, responsible, communicative message. Thinking so hard made him tired, so he put down the mike and lay on the couch to think some more. He thought so hard he fell asleep. He dreamed.

Coyote was trotting north. He was following an army of prospectors as they rushed toward Alaska for gold like insane lemmings. They shot at him when they saw him observing them— assholes!—so he stayed just far enough away, safe, curious and hungry. As they slowly struggled over icy mountain passes, they left in their tracks tremendous Coyote feasts of crippled, frozen horses. Finally the humans grew so cold and tired they stopped shooting at him, and Coyote got close enough to listen to their talk around their campfires. Their eyes shone with fever. Their voices spoke without laughter. They had one enflamed obsession, one golden topic of conversation. Soon, they had no energy even for talk, and clusters of frozen miners dotted the valleys. They burned each other's corpses in great roaring fires, as recorded by Robert Service.

With the tasty horsemeat gone, Coyote decided enough was enough, and turned back toward the south. But he was distracted from his course by the welcome sound of laughter. It was coming from round ice houses dotted along the snowfields. Coyote tiptoed up to one such house glowing with warmth like a lamp. He pressed his ear against the translucent snow blocks while the sled dogs slept buried in the snow beside him. Inside he heard parents telling sons and daughters and grandsons and granddaughters about the funny thing the club-footed boy did to the walrus. "'Look out! Klusiaq,*" said the boy, lying on his back and waving his big toe at the walrus, 'This toe eats monsters!'" The grandparents and sons and daughters-in-law and grandchildren all laughed and laughed while the tears ran down their cheeks, while their seal oil lamp burned low, while they ate their sealskin boots, while the single arctic dawn slowly raised itself over the mountains in barely perceptible increments of moons and menstrual cycles toward the rediscovery of hope. Coyote thought to himself, maybe I could live here after all. These folks are cool.*

Coyote woke. He was shivering. He threw the Navajo rug around his shoulders and reached for the microphone. He spoke clearly into its vibrating grains.

"You have reached the offices of the Coyote Cab Company and Travel Related Services. At the tone, please leave your name and number and the purpose of your call and I'll get back to you as soon as possible. Thank you very much for calling. Kindly leave your message now..." *BEEP.*

Coyote played it back. It communicated. It was professional. He liked it. He was impressed with himself. Yessir, a new day had dawned. No more screwing around. Down to business. Yessir.

On the way out the door he switched off the machine.

The next day the dust had settled. The office was empty. His briefcase was gone.

On the desk, the phone rang and rang and rang. And rang and rang again. Finally it stopped. Mavis Clovis, back from the jungle, the *Enquirer* folded in her hand, finally gave up. She couldn't get through.

Chapter 15
Coyote Has a Great Thing

Coyote was going along. Going through Central Park, he was, dragging his briefcase with one paw, chugging a Snickers bar with the other. It was hot and humid and the green trails under the oak trees were the coolest route to his next high-rise business appointment.

Coyote was as tired and unraveled as a mummy, but minding his own business, thinking to himself, Coyote, you have a Great Thing.

Here is a description of Coyote's Great Thing.

He and Thunderbird had just returned to the city from a whirlwind business trip. Hadn't slept in weeks. Been living on bottomless cups of truck stop coffee.

Coyote loved truck stops, particularly the waitresses at the Rainbow chain, who always gave him and the other guys a hard time while serving them like lightning. Coyote gave them a hard time too. Coyote was very good at giving out waitress hard times. It was one of his Great Things. But in the game of Coyote-waitress give and take, Rainbow waitresses were nonpareil.

"So Coyote, still driving that beater 'Bird, I see," one observed, wiping the counter with one hand and laying out a knife, fork, 'n spoon rolled in a paper napkin with the other. "That's OK, the rust goes good with your eyes," she added, sliding a glass of ice water down the Formica counter. She was right. Coyote's eyes were road-mapped with red highways and pitted as mufflers.

"Hey," retorted Coyote, "Why waste time on sleep when I'm on a roll, Mother? I got me a first class gig this time." He casually mentioned his latest whirlwind business trip to London, Paris, Rome, Luxembourg, and Tierra del Fuego. The waitress cocked a rainbow eye. She knew the Tierra del Fuego—a twenty-four-hour truck stop on the empty highway between El Paso and nowhere. She queried Coyote on his other fancy destinations. "Let me guess. London, Ontario; Paris, Texas; Rome, New York; Luxembourg, Wisconsin... am I right?"

She was right. More amazing, in the midst of her short repartee she had served Coyote two cups of coffee, real half & half in a metal pitcher, a plate of scrambled eggs with flecks of green peppers and red ham, wheat toast buttered and triangled, four strips of paper-thin—as opposed to lean—bacon, a cold glass of frozen orange juice, and three sprigs of parsley. She gave him the extra parsley because Coyote actually ate the stuff. He ate anything, and she noticed.

"OK, OK," said Coyote, "So North America is my territory. But don't let that news depress you. I'll be Coyote Worldwide soon."

"Hey," she said, sliding silently up the counter, "don't worry about me. Depression isn't in my job description. Each shift I gaze into the speedy eyes of a thousand truckin' travelers like you. I see a thousand jaws slapping up and down on meatball sandwiches and gravy. Everybody in a hurry to get somewhere or nowhere. I get to stay home. How could I get depressed? No, depression is a rich man's disease. Like you, Coyote," she said.

Coyote digested that last comment. Coyote, rich? Had to be a joke, right, another of the bon mots resulting from the Rainbow Truck Stop Waitresses' razor wit? Right?

Wrong. Coyote was on the make and making it big time this time. For his Great Thing he was working days, nights and weekends. Ignoring Coyote Woman, his fantasies, his children, his friends, his neighborhood, his house, his city, his country, his planet. His ninety-hour workweeks were legendary. Obviously, the word was out.

But who could have forecast the success of COYOTE MARKETING CONSULTANTS? Certainly not Coyote. All he did was print up some letterhead on Coyote Woman's laser printer and run a full-page ad on credit in the *Wall Street Journal.*

Coyote Woman thought he was joking. There he goes again, she said.

But the calls came in on the answering machine like a spring flood on the Missouri, like moonrise on the Bay of Fundy, like the eventual rotting and bursting of Hoover Dam.

It must have been the ad copy. One headline in extra-bold Futura type:

I HOLD THE KEYS TO THE UNIVERSE.
Coyote Marketing Consultants.
Call Toll Free.
1-800-COYOTES

When she heard the responses, Coyote Woman knew this indeed was a great thing. Damn, she said, why didn't I think of that? She set up a checking account, organized his appointment book, and sent him on the road.

Ever since then, Coyote and Thunderbird had been hot-rodding around the country from appointment to appointment. Consulting, Coyote had discovered, was hot business. Consultants had the answers, whatever the question. Coyote was providing answers by the trunkful to important people around the continent. People who would pay anything for advice, nothing for workers.

Advertising Directors wanted to demonstrate that ad campaigns could be successful within their Universe of

Prospects. Marketing Directors itched to discover what the Universe of Prospects was. Personnel Directors sought information on Employee Wellness and Universal Life Insurance. CEOs and Board Chairmen demanded guidance about Universal Takeover Trends—some wanted to grow their tiny conglomerates into the Biggest Corporation in the Universe, others hoped to just hold on to their bursting Corporate Universe a while longer. Religious evangelists, astrologers, and health food freaks wanted to check out competitive trends in the Fundamental Answers business. Psychiatrists and Psychologists needed to find out if someone had finally caught on.

Once he coaxed out the client's real problem, Coyote rummaged around in his briefcase or the trunk of the Thunderbird until he found something that addressed it.

Coyote had something for everyone, since he was always picking up Great Stuff wherever he went—along river banks, on mountain tops, in the middle of deserts, around northern lakes and ocean beaches, in wastebaskets, at garage sales, along trunk highways, in basements and attics of old houses, in the bags of bag ladies, in the hatbands of bag men.

He had the Great Thing that picked the lock of the client's insecurities. An unusual piece of river gravel with bright flecks in it indicated the Universe of Sales Prospects within the Universe of Sales Suspects. An old Inca *quipu*—a string of knotted cords—demonstrated the pathway toward a new inventory control system. A pine branch with an exceptional knurl in it showed the unexpected changes required in even the most careful Strategic Plan. A set of American Flag cuff links from a garage sale bolstered the Buy American theme badly needed by the shoe industry.

OK, OK, Coyote's approach was not original, he knew the Wizard of Oz had worked the same angle for years. But let's face it, it's a proven system. The bumbling insights of Oz had brought tears of gratitude to generations. And Coyote had millennia of similar experience. He had lots of Great Things. His appointment book ran the next seventeen weeks solid. Indeed, Coyote was rich.

So while Coyote dragged his briefcase through the park, he was exhausted but feeling good. Coyote, he said to himself, I think everybody is going to come up and say to me, "Aren't you Coyote? You have a Great Thing." Because, let's face it, you really do.

Without sleep for weeks, Coyote had cleverly propped open his eyelids with paper clips. But while reflecting so deeply on his Great Thing, he tripped on a tree root and the paper clips jumped out and his eyelids slammed down like heavy garage doors. He somnambulated off the path, slipped on fresh dog scat, fell into the warm grass under the cool shadow of a sycamore tree shadowed in turn by the mountains of surrounding high-rises, and slept like a stone.

He dreamed.

He was camping out alone. The Little Coyotes had scattered and the wind had swept his campsite clean and stomped his canoe and tangled his fishing line. But the storm had passed. He was sitting on a rock looking out over the lake, drying as it gleamed in the emerging sun.

Muskie had seen the whole sordid family affair and swam up to taunt him. "Hey Coyote," he shouted from the water, his needle-sharp teeth grinning, "Are you ever having a bad day!" "Me?" said Coyote, looking down at him. "I'm having a fine day, Muskie."

"No, you're not," chortled Muskie. "I saw what happened to you. And it's worse than you think. One of your Little Coyotes—the ones that fought so much and started your troubles...."

"Just scuffling," said Coyote. They'll get over it. It's good exercise." "Not all of them," laughed Muskie. "One jumped into the lake for a swim a while ago." "So?" said Coyote. "So, I just couldn't resist," riposted Muskie. "I had to eat him."

Coyote looked at him, incredulous. "Come on, Muskie, you don't expect me to believe that. Sure, you eat ducklings. I even heard tales of a poodle puppy, for which, if true, you have my congratulations. But a Coyote, even a pup? Forget it. You're not big enough."

"Am so," said Muskie, his monster jaws turning down in a kind of a pout. "I did so eat your Little Coyote. I had the worst time choking him down."

"Come on, Muskie. If you really ate a Coyote pup you'd have fur al over your teeth, and I don't see any."

Muskie wondered about that. "You're right. I certainly must have some fur on my teeth. Take a look, Coyote," and he swam closer to shore.

"I don't see any, Muskie. You're full of it, as usual."

Muskie swam closer. "Look way down my throat, Coyote. Maybe you can see a bit of furry tail. I feel it twitching down there."

"OK," said Coyote, "but I really have better things to do with this great afternoon. The sun is finally out and I want to lie around. You'll have to come in as close as you can. My eyes are sore with all the sand and rain and wind I got in them today." "Not to mention your bad luck," chuckled Muskie, and swam closer.

Before the echo of his laugh returned, Coyote flashed out a paw and knocked Muskie's tail onto the beach. Another paw knocked the rest of Muskie clean out of the water. He grabbed Muskie's huge flapping tail and held him up and shook him until Little Coyote slid out onto the shore, gasping for breath. "We'll figure out how to cook you later, Muskie buddy," said Coyote, throwing him into the cold firepit of the campsite.

Coyote picked up Little Coyote and held him in his arms. He was scared and trembling and extremely unhappy. Coyote carried him into the lake to wash him off. "Wait, Dad. Wait." "Don't be scared, Little One, I'll take care of you." "That's not it, Dad. My kit bag... don't get it wet." He unbuckled it from his waist and held it up. Coyote opened it. Inside were a terrycloth towel, two tin cups, a jug of cider, two sleeping bags, a pair of pajamas, a complete cooking kit, and matches. "Matches!" howled Coyote. He placed the bag on the shore, stepped into the clear water and gently washed the Little One head to toe, then dried him and fluffed him with the towel.

Then they roasted Muskie over a roaring fire. They laughed into the night. They knew Coyote Woman would never believe this Muskie story, true though it was.

Coyote woke up with the taste of fresh fishbones stuck in his mouth. He ached all over. His body felt like an intersection of slug slime trails at the racetrack. He sat up, grinding the sand dunes in his eyes. The hot summer park was thronged with people all exercising their Great Things:

Joggers. Bicyclists. Jugglers. Sleepers. Muggers. Walkers. Dancers. Drinkers. Pushers of baby strollers. Pushers of dope. Model boat sailors. Windsurfers. Roller skaters. Bench sitters. Race walkers. Picnickers with croissants and champagne. Artists. Tattoo artists. Panhandlers. Guys taking their shirts off and flexing. Tree climbers. Actors. Hair braiders. Canoeists. Bongo drummers. Soloists. Duets. Trios. Quartets. Orchestras. Family reunions. Grillers. Hot rodders. Black-leather motorcyclists. Skateboarders. Conversationalists. Designer Dress ladies. Briefcased men. Cruisers. Loners. Delivery guys. Boom-boxers. Bag ladies. Bag men.

"Look. Everybody has a Great Thing," said Coyote, slowly working the sleep sludge out of his joints. "Great. So do I."

“Aieeee,” he thought suddenly, “have I missed my appointment?” He eyed his wrist, slowly focusing on the fact that his wristwatch was missing. He stumbled to his paws. His wallet was gone. His briefcase was gone. His clothes were gone. Hey, his Snickers bar was gone! His appointment book was gone.

“Aieeee,” he howled, “I am naked! My Great Thing is stolen! What am I to do?”

He dragged himself over to the nearby reflecting pool, tears falling like high mountain streams from his swollen eyes. He splashed water onto his face, into his eyes, let it run off his nose. As the ripples settled on the surface of the pool, he watched his fuzzy form transform in front of him from a staccato burst of colorful random splashes into rough pulsating circles into a smooth wandering reflection.

Finally, gazing up at him was someone he recognized—Coyote, The Most Powerful Being on Earth (or at least in North America). Soft and furry and ragged as milkweed, a bedraggled tricky omnivore, opportunistic eater of berries and grasshoppers and rodents and house pets, a slipper of traps. Every bit as great as the day he was born.

“Hmm,” he said, and began to smile. As his lips parted his reflection revealed row upon row of shiny teeth, some flat as metates for grinding seeds and grain, others sharp as spikes to tear the flesh of watermelons and muskies and Chihuahuas. “Yes indeed,” he said, “I have a Great Thing.”

Coyote ambled toward home, his tail following along behind him.

He arrived to find a note.

Coyote:
You've been gone too long.
You've been gone much too long.
Baby I'm telling you, you've been gone too long.
The concert business is wired, and I'm sick of your song.
I'm off to a Hollywood party. If I see you again,
then it won't be sooooo loooong!
Coyote Woman

PS No time to lose, had to cash the consulting checks myself before anybody stopped payment. You did well, Coyote. I bought some dynamite earrings, and a turquoise necklace you would have wanted me to have. Plus, a turbo IBM laptop for the business. The rest barely covered an antique dress, a few shoes, a plane ticket, and a house.

PPS Leave the Keys to the Universe in the door.

Chapter 16
Coyote Deals With Stress

Coyote slyly observed her from across the room.

She had more stress fractures than the California coast. She was convinced her stomach was too large, her breasts too small, her hips too wide, her hair not shiny enough, her teeth too protrusive, her husband too intrusive. She was also convinced that she'd had First Person revelations about morality, work, child rearing, proper social and familial relations, house cleaning, disarmament, two-party politics, and the music business. Everything had to be Just Right.

Her name must be Stress.

Coyote, on the other hand, was cool. Relaxed. No jitters. No nerves. No problems. Whatsoever.

So what if he'd lost yet another job. He'd been there before, thousands of times. He was nothing if not resourceful. A new entrepreneurial scheme—microcomputers for trees—was already brewing in his flaming consciousness.

After the collapse of his consulting empire and the departure of his family without a trace, he recalled with fondness the cool embrace of the sycamore as he napped in the park for what must have been weeks. He wondered who was looking out for the trees' interests.

A whirlwind market research trip to forests around the continent, during which he interviewed thousands of trees about their computational, word processing, and spreadsheet needs, revealed that trees have a vested interest in the computer revolution, leading, as it can, to the "paperless office." Get it? No paper, no trees to be cut down and, gag, beaten to pulp. Coyote got it.

His new trade association, We Speak for Trees, already had an 800 number and was lobbying its first bill in Washington, mandating electronic storage for all federal records and the elimination of paper files.

He was having some trouble organizing the redwoods and western red cedars on the issue, who told him, Let's face it, we have a different set of problems. Ever heard of lumber??? But the alders and aspens and birches and basswoods all signed up immediately, with handsome fees paid in advance. The trip was a success.

Feeling powerful, he accepted the challenge of calming the woman across the room. He would bring her to her senses. Love her into relaxation. Trip her up with kindness. Insist on humor no matter what the provocation. Turn her on to the Coyote Way.

He watched her maneuver across the crowded room, a mug of sassafras root beer in his hand, some apparently expensive Chardonnay in hers. Her hair was radiant, with streaks of sun-rich accents against the thick dark roots below. Her dress was daring—an antique bright rayon print out of the forties, black and red, accented with a magenta sash belt and silver hoop earrings. Turquoise, jet, and freshwater pearls hung off her neck like so many fish. Earthy. She carried her body like a dancer, straight, insouciant, but with a firmness underneath. And at this distance, he felt that her skin was the consistency of sour cream. Smoother than silk, softer than down, cooler than gold. And she was, or so it seemed, unattached. He watched her in conversation over by the fireplace, etching numerous eager admirers with acid repartee.

He made his move.

She saw him advancing toward her out of the corner of her eye. She paused in mid-sentence in the process of putting down some petty film director or other, and turned to look directly at him. Her eyes! Big as a sunset, yellow and sharp as dry California grass.

She appeared to recognize him.

"Is that you, Coyote?" she said, her mouth and eyebrows defining a new interpersonal doctrine of benign contempt.

"*Pardonnez-moi*," said Coyote, "are *vous* speaking to *moi*?"

She can't possibly recognize me, Coyote thought to himself, his confident hustle barely slowed. This disguise is my best to date.

Indeed, he looked good. The shades, the beret, his hair matted into dreadlocks, the baggy pants, the suspenders, the loose-fitting woodblock print shirt, the North African sandals made from old Michelin tires. He was nothing if not continental, completely masking his native Coyote nature.

Already he had regaled several women at the party with his European escapades and broad internationalist perspective. They hung on each pinched off syllable, unaware of his private joke. He didn't know up from down about Europe, not to mention Asia, Africa, or Antarctica. His only continent was this one, America, North and South. But he knew America never played well at sophisticated, coastal, big-city parties like this one, so he floated his Parisian hot air attitude. American as he was, Coyote was Coyote. He had other agendas as well. Women were one.

Women. What a fantastic invention. Sometimes he thought he had invented them himself. As he stepped further across the room, he licked his lips and closed his eyes. He dreamed.

Coyote took a clump of warm desert mud after a rainstorm and rolled it between his paws, the soft silken mud, and shaped it the way his dream thought it should be shaped, roundnesses and fullnesses here and indentations there, and covered it with the glorious petals of blooming desert plants until she shimmered and glowed with a multicolored radiance, and then Coyote set her free under the high arc of an impossible triple rainbow and she stood regal and sensuous on the bank of the spectacular desert arroyo just hinting at its later magnificence when it became known as the Grand Canyon. And a shaft of sunlight burned down upon her.

He saw it coming, saw the shaft of laser sunlight pierce the heart of the triple rainbow and race toward her and in an instant there would be illumination and this fearsome inexplicable itch he had been having for years now, centuries now, millennia now, would finally be fulfilled, her soft cloudlike glory would be suffused over him and his nights and days would be animated with endless new possibilities.

And then he noticed. Spines. Little shiny tips of sharp cactus spines protruding out of the mud.

Oh no, he had made an error. In the exuberance of creation, he did not inspect the initial desert mud closely. Spines. Cactus spines. Oh no.

He looked up. The shaft of sunlight was on its way, unstoppable. He looked at the light, the petals, the light, the silken mud, the light, the spines. Oh no. At the last possible second, he dove to intercept the shaft, to take it, if he had to, in his own eye!

He missed. Instead, he launched himself over the edge of the arroyo, tumbling through space toward the tiny creek meandering like a silver snake below.

As he tumbled, he heard two things.

First, the flash flood. It was roaring. The roaring of all the caged beasts of the jungle. The roaring of all the waterfalls on the continent. The roaring of all the high-speed traffic on the freeways.

He saw the wall of water towering over him. The front wave curled like the Banzai pipeline, but full of scouring rocks and boulders and gravel and sand, not to mention thousand-year-old bristlecone pines, pinyon pines, saguaro cacti, prickly pears, Gila monsters, sidewinders, tarantulas, black widows, scorpions, and red ants by the billions.

If only he could swim.

At the last nanosecond, before the wave engulfed him and he helped, in an accidental sort of way, create the Grand Canyon, Coyote heard something else. A laugh.

He glanced up. The shaft of sunlight had split the rainbows into a sky full of iridescent colors, the entire heavens a rainbow palette of primaries and secondaries and tertiaries.

And she was standing there, a splendor covered in a gown of desert blossoms. Her head tilted back, her night sky hair streaming out behind her, her shiny, warm brown skin glowing like a commercial. She was illuminated with pollen, strong and bright and powerful. And she was laughing out loud.

And here she was before him.

He looked through his shades. He knew she knew.

"Hello, Stressie. Miss me?" Coyote asked.

"Coyote Woman to you, asshole," she answered.

It was obvious she hadn't.

Chapter 17
Coyote Hosts All Night Talk Radio

"Hello, you're on the air. What's on your mind?"

"Hello? Hello? Is this Coyote? Am I on the air? Did I actually get through?"

"Uh, turn your radio down, will you Miss, you're getting a delay... that's it. Now, that should be better...."

These bozos, Coyote thought to himself. They listen to all night talk radio their whole adult lives. Dream of getting on the air to hang out their psychic underwear. And yet they never figure out how it's done. Technically speaking. It was beginning to piss him off.

"Ohhh, Coyote, is it really you? The Most Famous Radio Host on Earth (or at least in North America)? I'm soooo excited!"

Yes, Coyote was famous again. All Night Talk Radio, the COYOTE NETWORK, syndicated throughout North

America and picked up in South America as well through simultaneous translation into Spanish, Nahuatl, Portuguese, Quechua, Navajo, Hopi, Lakota, Anishinabe, Iroquois, Araucanian, Aymara, and others.

Coyote was a hit. And he was getting pooped.

All night he'd sit on his butt, one AM to Sunrise, seven days a week, the big mike on the desk in front of him. He'd alternately listen to the stories of listeners and tell stories of his own. He was beginning to miss just a hint of fresh air and actual physical movement. His sense of proportion was growing curiouser and curiouser. His sense of humor was going daffy.

Coyote leaned back in his swivel chair. It was raining outside the studio. He could see the silver drops running down the sealed double-pane skylight glass overhead. He missed the rain.

He remembered nostalgically his original studio. Not much. The studio in a cave, the transmission tower a piece of scavenged copper wire lashed to a ponderosa pine, power provided by an electric generator turned by a mountain stream.

The communication business seemed a good idea at the time. A buzz. A lark. And anyway, it was night work, which suited his metabolism. His eclectic pirate radio format was an instant success, bringing in fat sponsors to negotiate with Coyote Enterprises, until an indignant beaver gnawed down the pine and Coyote had to sell out.

Now his program was part of a big city radio conglomerate with studios on the top floor of a tall city skyscraper. They signed him up fast with a tight contract negotiated by Coyote Woman. Now he never got outside. He was too successful. Indispensable as the North Star. Here's the secret of his success.

Coyote was a good listener and a natural storyteller. Every night he wove together complex plots and eccentric characters and ancient dreams. He ignored reality. All Night Talk Radio was no place for reality. Fantasy and good taste were the only criteria, the first required by the audience, the second by the FCC.

Coyote knew his audience. Having been out at night off and on for millennia, he understood night people.

Not the insomniacs. They are night people by accident, not by design.

Not the predators either. They are too busy catching rodents and stealing candelabras and beating little old ladies and brewing ferocious drugs to have any time to dream at night. They dream during the day. Coyote wasn't on the air then, so he couldn't help.

But the ordinary people who tune into All Night Talk Radio in their lonely houses and huts and apartments and shelters and lay there in the glow of the clock radio or the red "on" light of the transistor sister or its further electronic iterations—these he held in the palm of his paw.

They projected themselves out of the confined universe of their rotten husbands and shitty lovers and bawling kids and sick mothers and lousy jobs and finally after the booze and the beatings and the diapers and the crying and the back pain they lay down and it was QUIET, FINALLY and they could hear themselves breathing, slower and slower, finally in a deep slow rhythm and then the tight synapses of the rotten day would slowly unravel and they would begin to reach out, just a little, then completely as the night progressed, reach out into the universe of radio waves and listen to their fellow desperate day creatures lay their dreams across the ionosphere and Coyote would tell them wily stories and listen to their own sad tales until the sun rose in the east of the Western Hemisphere and it was time again for the breakfast and the beatings and the booze and the crying kids and the rotten daycare and the bag lunch and the sewing machine and the assembly line and the flat tires and the broken lawnmower and the tourists with cameras and the weaving with sticks and the price rises on kerosene and the dry holes for the corn seed and the broken pumps and the greasy hands and the hounding landlord and the murderous comrades and the gathering of firewood and the cooking of corn and the pouch of peas and the fish sticks and tortillas and guinea pigs and the sun is down again finally so wrap in the poncho and the sheets and the children gather in your bed and rustle under the blankets and it's a body pile of squirming and fighting and then a body pile of twitching warmth and then they are relaxed and gone and then you can plug in again to the high hemispheric network of COYOTE ALL NIGHT TALK RADIO. Thank God.

Maybe that is why Coyote was beginning to feel so uncomfortable. For millennia his schtick was offbeat antics, scrambler, teacher, creator, fool. Now his listeners were viewing him as The Real Thing. A God.

God is not an easy job, he knew.

Once God is your job, work becomes burdensome. He was losing his sense of humor. Spinning out of control. He had just told over the airwaves a series of highly questionable jokes and was bound to be in big trouble with the FCC. The jokes went like this.

I imagine you are sitting there wondering, radio listeners, how humor first entered the world. What, for example, was the First Joke in the World? Well, Coyote was there. The first joke went like this.

These two big Clovis guys, see, are having a disagreement around the campfire and are banging each other over the head with big tree branches while a bunch of other guys are standing around watching and scratching. The branches rise and fall in big slow arcs—whoosh, whoosh—*that soften the impact due to all the small branches and leaves catching the wind. Bark is flying and leaves are rattling but neither adversary is doing any real damage. Finally, one of the guys stops the proceedings. "Wait a minute, wait a minute. We're not getting anywhere. Gather round," he says, "I have an idea." He takes one of the big branches and strips off the rest of the bark and the smaller branches and leaves and breaks off the thin wimpy end and takes a rock and pounds and shapes the remaining branch into a thinner end for a handle and a rounded heavier end for striking. When he's finished, he puts it down on the ground and the rest of the guys gather in a big circle and put their long hairy arms around one another and admire this seminal creation. "Hey," says one of them, "we ought to get together like this once a month. We've formed a club!"*

Howwwwl! Yip yip yip! Get it? Formed a club! The first pun! The first war club! And the first Kiwanis Club! Hysterical, yes???

No? Well, the other Clovis guys didn't get it either. But I was there, hanging around the outside of the campfire—where New Mexico is now—and when I heard them say this thing, why, I just broke up. I howled and howled. They nearly jumped out of their mammoth skins. By the way, this joke is also told about Neanderthals, I hear.

So call me with your nominations for the earliest jokes in the world. In the meantime, here's another early one that comes to mind.

So Grok was out hunting this mastodon, see. And he finally brings it down with his best spear. Well, just then a snowstorm comes up and it gets very cold. So, Grok slices open the belly of the mastodon and crawls in to keep warm and outlast the storm. Well, the storm turns out to be an Ice Age. Lasts 20,000 years. The Wisconsin glaciation. Finally it ends. Ten or so thousand years later a paleontologist comes upon the mastodon frozen in the North American tundra. He writes about it in a scholarly journal and the newswires pick it up which brings in electronic media from all over the world who come up to see the unveiling of the frozen mammoth. OK? So, the paleontologist says to himself, I have to come up with something that will catch the attention of these television guys. So in front of the hot lights of the assembled TV cameras and commentators, the paleontologist lights a small charcoal grill, then takes out his knife and slices off a bit of Mastodon meat. And starts frying it up in front of the television audience. He's about to take a bite when Grok jumps out from the inside. "Hey," he says, "this is my kill! Get yer own fuckin' mastodon!"

Yip! Yip! Yip! "Get yer own fuckin' mastodon!!!!!" Howwwwl!!!!!!!

Coyote fell off his chair and was thrashing on the floor in front of his microphone, crying with laughter. He slowly composed himself and sat back up, weak and exhausted, wiping tears from his eyes and soaked whiskers, and checked back in with his caller on line one.

"So. You get it turned down yet?" Coyote gasped. "OK, you're on All Night Talk Radio. Yes, this is Coyote himself. Who else? So, what are you dreaming about?"

"First," said the caller, "Coyote, you just can't tell jokes like that on the air. That mastodon business. The FCC is going to be all over your case. You used the F-word, Coyote. That's a no-no. You're finished in broadcasting. Not to mention that those jokes were lousy. All that 'whooshing' for a dumb 'club' pun? You're losing it, Coyote. Time to move on. Before you really embarrass yourself in front of the people who love your stories."

"Stop hassling me, lady," snapped Coyote. "So, I'm a little off. It's the air. Stuffy in here. No light. No stars. But now it's your turn. Tell us your story, please. And relax." But he himself didn't feel relaxed. He *was* losing it. He had just joked himself off the air. Why did he ever tell jokes? He was lousy at jokes! Stick to stories!

The station manager was desperately signaling him from the engineer's booth. Drawing his finger across his throat, telling him to end the show. FCC commissioners were lighting up the lines.

Too late. Her story was underway.

"I know a secret place," she said, lowering her voice, "where twice five miles of fertile ground with walls and towers are girdled round. And there are gardens bright with sinuous rills, where blossom many an incense-bearing tree, and there are forests ancient as the hills, enfolding sunny spots of greenery."

"You do?" said Coyote. "Sounds wonderful. Tell us more." He proffered his middle claw to the sweating station manager.

"Yes, yes," said the voice, now becoming hauntingly familiar. "With caves of ice. And Alph the sacred river ran through caverns measureless to man, down to a sunless sea. And the shadow of a dome of pleasure floats midway on the waves."

Coyote was becoming giddy, the microphone seeming to float away in front of him. Whatever a pleasure dome was, it loomed before him in the studio like a vibrant egg.

She continued in a hush. "But oh, that deep romantic chasm which slanted down the green hill athwart a cedern cover. A savage place! As holy and enchanted as e're beneath a waning moon is haunted... by woman wailing for her demon-lover!" And the voice trailed off into a soft moan.

"Ahhhhh..." sighed Coyote. "Ahhhhh..." sighed the radio audience around the Western Hemisphere in spinal response to Coleridge's romantic tale.

At the instant of the collective sigh, the wind rustled up off the dirty bedroom floors and raced through the high-rises and the trees and the jungles of eyes and the streets of rain and the caverns of rivers and the peaks of clouds and the pits of despair. And howled.

Ahhhhhhhhh...

And the ionosphere collapsed. Behind its sheltering blanket the high black night roared with points of stars, each with its own universe of stories, its own households of needs deeper than wells. And its own jokes. Better jokes. Older jokes. And all the radios in the world went dead.

On the street, Coyote danced and howled in the streaming rain. Mavis Clovis had finally gotten through.

Chapter 18
Coyote and the Attack of the Downers

Getting fired from talk radio came as no shock to Coyote. Even Coyote Woman didn't mind. She happened to be working late and caught his infamous last show. Clearly, Coyote was losing it. Time for something new. So, she brought him home for a rest at her house high in the Hollywood Hills. The Little Coyotes might like to see him too. Especially Baby Coyote, who had just dropped in from the clouds in a rare LA rainstorm gushing happily about her extensive bunny experiences.

After all that studio work, Coyote's muscles and lungs cried out for fresh oxygen, not LA exhaust. Not to mention that his feet itched for the open road. Not to mention that the low poetic growl of a woman wailing for her demon lover was driving him mad with itching down his back. But Baby Coyote was back! He couldn't wait to hug her.

But once in the house, the incessant click of his toenails on the polished hardwood floors plus the rasping as he scratched his itch on the doorjambs was driving Coyote Woman and the Little Coyotes crazy. The Little Ones headed for the streets and alleys to play ball and invent computer games and produce digital cartoons. Meanwhile, Mrs. C. was welded to the phone trying to bag a warm-up comedy act for the Solstice Show. No one was striking her as funny.

So she wasn't displeased when Coyote applied for a job as a roadie with the circus, taking an eager Baby Coyote along with him. She could get much more work done, she said. She was also thinking of a chaperone. No telling when a poetry-moaning woman would catch sight of Coyote's laid-back ears.

When the black-hatted Ringmaster grinned his toothy assent over the phone, Coyote was delighted. He and Baby Coyote and Thunderbird hit the road to Chicago to meet the circus train like lovers on a first overnight date.

Baby Coyote snuggled into Coyote's lap in the Thunderbird driver's seat, gurgling a wide smile. Coyote hugged her tight while both of them closed their eyes and held their noses high through the passing landscape redolent with summer hay and wildflower perfume.

Don't be scared, Coyote isn't driving any more. The Thunderbird was riding on a flatbed train car in the circus caravan, hurtling through the fresh-cut alfalfa fields in the midsection of America. He was earning cheeseburgers and cherry pie and coffee and milk in the mess tent and a paycheck to boot by setting up and tearing down the high wire. He also performed low level comedy between circus acts. The Ringmaster was desperate due to an inexplicable outbreak of the D (Downer) virus infecting the clown population. Baby Coyote was an integral part of Coyote's routine.

"What a great way to see the continent," Coyote thought to himself as he snuggled Baby Coyote and sniffed the air for alfalfa incense and kept a sharp eye out for gardens bright with sinuous rills. And who knew what savage storytellers might attend the Greatest Show on Earth.

The circus pulled into the outskirts of a midwestern city late that night. "Where are we this week?" wondered the groggy circus workers as they rolled out of the sleeping cars. Coyote certainly didn't know. He helped set up the high wire for the day's performance, didn't finish until sunrise. He was pooped—hey, this was hard work!

As he stumbled off toward the pup tent he shared with Baby Coyote, the sun crested over the eastern horizon. Coyote squinted. He had a sudden creepy feeling that he'd been to this place before. There was something familiar about that black building etched against the emerging orange glow with its huge black smokestack sucking at the sun like a straw, sucking the life out of the sky. Coyote's back fur rose involuntarily as if he'd seen sign of a marauding wolf pack. And he had. For this was the home of The Downers.

The Down-looking Family was the most vicious archenemy Coyote had ever faced. Seven strong—Mom, Dad, Uncle, Aunt, three ageless kids, two girls and a boy, or two boys and a girl—all with frozen limbs and grinding jaws. They shuffled relentlessly. They shuffled through the park kicking dead leaves, across the street counting bubblegum splats, across the terrazzo floor of their homes swirling dustballs, along the margins of clear lakes dragging cold sand. They were on the trail of Coyote. They were determined to rub him out.

"Aieeee!!! What am I to do?" wailed Coyote, pacing around and around the tent. "I am camped in the front yard of my arch enemies, but Baby Coyote is sound asleep inside. What am I to do?"

He crawled into the tent to think some more and found Baby Coyote snorting and giggling in the midst of a delighted dream. He snuggled her tightly into his arms, her warmth comforting the chill in his heart. He pulled the sleeping bag up over both of them and thought some more, gazing out the flap of the tent as the orange of sunrise turned pink, then purple, then blue.

He fell asleep. He dreamed.

He was traveling with Baby Coyote asleep in his arms, stumbling through a thick steaming fertile ground athwart a cedern cover, a southern northern jungle decorated with flickers and parrots and cedars and pines and vines. Sweet syrupy incense swirled through his nostrils as he emerged into a sunny cove of greenery with turtles nesting in the sand. Coyote tingled with excitement. But then, out of the surrounding green sinuous rills a huge black smokestack rose up and pierced the sky. The Down-looking Family emerged from the smokestack like a phalanx of slugs and slowly slimed toward him, consuming the forest as they moved. Coyote was paralyzed by their deep rhythmic breathing, the crescendo of their shuffling feet, the dust clouds rising up behind them blocking out the sun and Baby Coyote's dreams, drying up her brain, blowing away her laugh like a wisp of wicked witch's hair.

He woke up with a sweaty moan.

He looked out through the flap of the tent into the noise and bright lights of the Big Top. The circus was starting up. Barkers were barking, contortionists stretching, horses and tigers dancing. Time to go to work. It was only a dream. Coyote relaxed.

Then dark shadows fell across the tent. Heavy feet stood in front of the open flap. They were all shuffling. They were all raising dust. Coyote recognized those feet.

Coyote felt the hair on his back rise up around him like an electric halo as he reached instinctively to protect the warm sleeping fluff of Baby Coyote in the curl of his arms. They were trapped like mice. And in the rising dust, Coyote felt he was going to sneeze.

But the Downers passed by. Two new feet suddenly arrived, covered with sensible white shoes and white stockings. They urged the other feet along. The heavy shoes slowly turned and shuffled toward the barkers of the Big Top, leaving a cloud of dust behind them and a cold chill covering Coyote's ventricles like a cholesterol blanket. He hugged Baby Coyote tightly to him. He hacked and coughed and perspired.

Coyote and Baby Coyote emerged from the tent. It was time for their act.

Coyote was badly rattled. Fortunately, his circus performance did not require much concentration. Pure filler. His job was to buy relaxation time for an audience rendered limp and perspiring by the death-defying gyrations of the previous amazing act prior to their thunderstruck attention to the impossibly dangerous act to follow.

Immediately preceding Coyote had been the justly acclaimed Irenia Valisnokov Karasovich, known as the Great Pretzel. She had an immense talent. She tied herself in knots, smoked cigarettes with her toes, stood on her elbows, dangled by her teeth and spun around until the stands were roaring with the impossibility of such spinning, hundreds of times at incredible rpms, the crowd counting in unison three hundred, four hundred, five hundred, and finally after torturing them to their ecstatic peak she somehow put on the brakes by arching her back even further and stopped and climbed down and bowed to the four directions, and with each bow her marvelous spangled cleavage drooped open revealing huge soft couches of comfort, while simultaneously behind her a spangled derriere popped up to the opposite audience revealing a back and hips and thighs and knees and ankles and hamstrings so impossibly supple as to excite even preadolescent boys into roars of excitement and approval and anticipation.

After her, the place was exhausted. It was Coyote's job to bring them back to life.

Generally, he was good at it. He'd step out into the ring of light wearing a spangled red, white, and blue tuxedo, topped off with a red, white, and blue top hat—the Ringmaster insisted on that—bottomed off with his black high-top sneakers—Coyote insisted on those. He would survey the crowd. He would slowly smile—a large, toothsome smile. Then he would take Baby Coyote out from inside his coat and hug her, and she would gurgle with pleasure. Then he would hold her up, and tickle her, and she would laugh. Then he would throw her up in the air. Baby Coyote loved being thrown up in the air. And she would laugh out loud. And everybody in the stands would laugh involuntarily.

Coyote's secret was that the audience could hear every murmur Baby Coyote made through a microphone pinned underneath the bib at her chin. The sound was piped through a powerpack transmitter strapped on Coyote's back right into the gigawatt public address system of the Big Top and from there into the individual ears and deep mammalian memory banks of the spectators. They were no longer spectators, but participants. They were instantly reminded that they too were mammals. That they bear their young alive and hold them close and feed them milk from their breasts. That they rear them for an impossibly long time with close and loving attention. Those helpless, dependent babies repay that love with gurgles and smiles and laughter.

It was a routine known to parents and older siblings and grandparents and babysitters around the planet. Coyote spread the simple infection of laughter until the whole audience rollicked with the joyful hormones of a contented baby trilling in their ears.

Except the Downers. They didn't know how to laugh. And they were in the audience today.

They didn't know how to laugh because they never heard the baby. They were unable to pay attention outside of themselves. Their limits of perception and patience and tolerance had snapped. Their dreams had blown up in their faces like faulty household furnaces. They were burned all over the insides of their skulls. Their arms were frozen to their chests in stifled snapped rage. They wore old tentlike housedresses and strolled around the grounds of their institutions cursing out loud or silently sobbing. And they only looked down.

They were taken to the circus in a formal institutional effort at amusement. No chance. They were shot. And their icy energy was dedicated to shooting Coyote.

Coyote felt the hush of ten thousand lungs after Irenia Valisnokov Karasovich had driven the entire Big Top mad with her spinning. Everybody, that is, except the Downers. For the first time in his life, Coyote felt infected with the D virus: doubt, depression, despair, and looming disaster. It was only a hint of what the Downers felt. The cold wind of circumstance and attitude and accident and failure and misery and grief had brought them rats in the night and rats in the daytime and rats that had eaten their hopes bite after bite and finally their hopes were gone and they were Downers and they could only look down.

He knew they were poisoning the bleachers. He knew the amazing spins of Irenia Valisnokov Karasovitch had caused them no stirring. He knew that the crushed popcorn under the wooden seats was more fascinating than the spinning of a Goddess. He knew they would not be looking at him. They were sucking the life out of the Big Top and he couldn't stop it.

What should he do? Coyote looked into the pool of light in front of him, his fur underneath his red, white, and blue spangled coat standing up straight against the ice-cold chill tumbling down from the Downers' cheap seats like a breeze off glaciers. He couldn't get them out of his mind.

Instead of pouncing into the light in the center ring, he found his feet heavy as stones. He could not lift them. He shuffled into the circle of light, one thick foot at a time, Big Top dust rising in a cloud around him.

He sneezed in the rising dust. An explosion echoed through the PA system. He looked up, his eyes beginning to water. Then his lapel sneezed. Or so it seemed to the audience. The audience stirred a little. He looked down at his coat. Then he sneezed again, a louder, sort of a snapping whoop. His lapel followed with a whoop of its own. The audience murmured with surprise. He reached for his handkerchief, a four-foot square red bandana that he used as a bib and blew his nose. Then he reached in and his lapel blew its nose. The audience stirred with involuntary chuckles. Coyote began to feel better.

The cold breeze, the Downers' chill, was still falling around him, but at least he had time. The doubt in his heart was loosening. He decided to pounce.

Baby Coyote hung on tight to his fur as he suddenly dashed out of the light in the center of the ring and raced up the bleacher stairs. The surprised spotlight man followed him as best he could. Coyote stopped at the row of the Downers, who all sat inspecting shoe-level gum wrappers.

Their nurse attendant drew a huge breath, a wind tunnel sucking sound, but he picked the Downers up one at a time and pounced them quickly to the top of the Big Top where the high wire stretched over the center ring.

He placed them on the tiny platforms, four at each end, with only a wire between them. No net. They stood there on those tiny platforms, looking down over their shoe tops. And there below them were three round rings, surrounded by clowns and circled with prancing horses.

Coyote slid down the wire and dropped again into the circle of light in the center ring. And he began to smile. And when he paused to blow his nose with his huge red handkerchief, the whole audience stirred again. And when he blew the nose of his lapel, the place began to laugh. He stood there, a huge toothy smile on his face, his nose running like a waterfall.

And when he finally pulled Baby Coyote from beneath his coat, and she hugged him, and he held her up, and she smiled her huge toothy, runny-nose smile, and he threw her up and she giggled, the organist went wild and reached into the memory bank of his high school piano class and broke into "Jesu, Joy of Man's Desiring," while the whole audience began a rhythmic joyful swaying and foot-stomping.

But Coyote was still afraid to look all the way up. Even as he held up Baby Coyote and tickled her, and threw her high, then threw her higher until she nearly touched the high wire and her lapel mike sent her joyous trilling laughter into the gigawatt PA system and into the individual ears and memories of the entire Big Top and the whole place dissolved in laughter, he was afraid to look up.

But finally he did. And for the first time, for anybody's first time since they became Downers, someone was looking them straight their eyes. And they were looking straight at a desperately howling fool, a flood out of every orifice, and at Baby Coyote, laughing herself into delighted tears as she rose and fell, rose and fell, just below their shoe tops.

There was nothing more that he could do.

Coyote and Baby Coyote left the ring to a rain of warm applause. The Ringmaster rushed up to him with a contract for the full season. But Coyote collected his pay and quit. He and Thunderbird and Baby Coyote left that black smokestack in a cloud of dust and didn't stop driving until the mountains and canyons of home came into view.

Chapter 19
No Rain on Coyote's Parade

It was to be his first parade as a candidate. The Campaign Kick-off, Coyote Woman told him. Everyone would be watching. He would drive around the entire country in one day, sunrise to sunset, touching some place important to everybody. The crucial media event in his campaign.

Hey, Coyote was into it. He loved parades. It was only the rest of the stuff that had him a little concerned.

Coyote was running for President. Of the United States. Of North America.

How did he get into this?

When the Party Honchos visited his place and asked him to run, he said "Run? I'm good at running. Been all over the place. Can go forever."

"We know," they said. "And we also know that everybody likes you, unless they know you, and not very many people actually know you."

"Hey!" said Coyote.

"What we mean is, you're a myth. What a career you've had! Creator. Trickster. Cult leader. Rock star. Marketing guru. Entrepreneur. Radio host. Circus clown. You have great power. And you have humor, a commodity our pollsters tell us is of much more electoral value than commonly appreciated. And you'd make a hell of a media personality. You can win. You should be our Candidate for President."

Coyote Woman interrupted immediately. "He'll do it," she said.

"What?" said Coyote.

"He'll do it," she said. "Now go away so we can plan the campaign," she said and ushered the Party Honchos out the door.

"What?" said Coyote.

"I'll be your Campaign Manager," Coyote Woman said. "These guys will raise the bucks. Which won't be a problem, with party designation, because you are indeed a marketable commodity. Why didn't I think of it?"

"What?" said Coyote.

"OK, brush your teeth and let's get moving. They'll go out and open the campaign office. I'm going to put together a Parade."

"Then what?" said Coyote.

"You just wait and see," said Coyote Woman.

The parade across the country in one day was a stroke of organizational and media genius. Coyote was to drive the Thunderbird from the Atlantic coast's urban canyons through suburban arroyos and exurban gardens and rural fields down to swampy Caribbean bayous, then up green valleys and dusty prairies to the Great Lakes, then to the Black Hills and down along the Continental Divide, through the Grand Canyon and the Valley of the Shadow of Death and on to the Pacific coast, all beneath a celebratory hail of shredded bond orders, wadded up grocery bills, torn up grain receipts, falling water, and trees and rocks and gravel and sand and shells.

The only thing that could kill it was rain.

But the sky over North America on NATIONAL COYOTE PARADE DAY was as blue as a white man's eyeball, as pale and as high. The vault of the sky was solid and consistent as machine-dyed fabric. Not a cumulus. Not a horse's tail. Not a hole. Not a seam.

Coyote and his red '56 Thunderbird ate a lot of dust that day, starting with orange juice and coffee and bagels and blintzes in the deep shadows of New York City at first light and ending at a crazed celebrity rock and roll and beansprout bash on the Santa Monica pier at sunset (Elvis and Patsy Cline and Dylan and Prince were said to be there). He made a huge national media impression by dancing wildly at both parties. In between, local cameras caught him touching the rocks, soil, trees, and water sources of most every hometown on the continent.

At the end of the day, he was pooped, to be sure. His tongue hung out like an artist's canvas covered with pastels of dust. The passenger seat of the Thunderbird was filled with choked air filters. But he and Thunderbird were instantly famous.

All the TV stations covered it live, because Coyote looked great in the Thunderbird making gravel tracks around America. All the radio stations carried it, thanks to Coyote's former affiliations with All Night Talk Radio. All the important national newspapers—the *Enquirer*, the *Star*, the *Weekly world News*—gave it front page prominence because it met their editorial criteria: new, unusual, would fascinate the public, no content required.

And no content was served up. All debate invitations and policy questions were fended off by Coyote Woman, who was as organized and deft as a ballet dancer.

Coyote continued to rise in the polls day after day, week after week, month after month.

He won the party nomination in a landslide.

For his acceptance speech, Coyote stepped up to the convention podium and waved while the band played and the berserk delegates stomped and howled, festooned with Coyote buttons and Coyote noses and Coyote ears. He was cool as a cucumber, but Coyote Woman was nervous as a cat. This was the only unprogrammed moment in the campaign. She had tried to tell him what to say, had a complete text written out, then an outline, at least a note card, but Coyote paid no attention.

He wasn't worried, he said, a story would come to him. But what story? That worried Coyote Woman a lot. And now he was up there with no notes, without a net. She hoped at least there were a few jokes in it. But only tasteful jokes. No puns. No profanity. She paced the control booth like a caged hyena.

As the applause and band finally subsided, Coyote stepped up to the microphone. He tilted his head back and closed his eyes. This is the story he told.

THE BIRTH OF COYOTE

Before the Earth was born, the Coyote People lived in darkness. They lived by touching each other. And they were happy. And they tumbled through empty darkness in a big furball.

This is the Way it Had Always Been.

Then Mother Coyote began to swell. What is happening to me? she asked as she felt the beginning roundness of her belly. The other Coyote People felt of it, this graceful roundness. It must be something wonderful, they said.

And she grew bigger and bigger. And then her round soft belly began to move. Feel this, she exclaimed, and the Coyote People, one by one, put their soft paws, and then their ears, on Mother Coyote's womb. They felt fast running feet. They heard incipient jokes, wisecracks, and questions one after the other.

Ahh, they said, this will be a Great Thing.

And they continued to tumble through time, wondering and waiting for Something To Happen.

Mother Coyote felt an enormous pressure. It was a pressure from outside herself. It was a pressure from deep inside her. It was a pressure so startling in its intensity and so miraculous in its combination of crippling pain and ecstatic pleasure that she could in no way describe it. Something is about to happen, is all she could say.

And something did happen.

There was an explosion. An explosion which created light. An explosion which created matter. An explosion which created time.

An explosion which created Coyote.

He was launched through space, alone, nearly forever. He was warm in his soft fur coat, and to pass the time he entertained himself by telling stories.

Around him gases congealed into great swirling soups of dust, which congealed into galaxies, which exploded into red giants and white dwarfs and which contracted into stars which spun into fragments of molten matter which cooled into ice balls and fireballs and furballs.

Coyote landed on his back on one small furball. He called it Turtle Island. He called it Earth. He called it Home.

"It's a pleasure to be here," said Coyote.

Coyote stopped speaking. He opened his eyes and looked around.

He smiled and sat down.

The huge auditorium crowd remained silent. Waiting for an ending, no doubt. Or at least a policy statement. Or a joke. But that was it.

Coyote Woman, eyes rolling, signaled the band, which quickly broke into the Beatles' "Let It Be." A masterful stroke.

The whole convention slowly rose and rocked back and forth in unison, an entire generation of delegates and television viewers bathing itself in nostalgic tears. And drowning Coyote in applause.

There was no rain on coyote's parade. And according to the next day's polls, he was a shoo-in to win the Presidency.

Chapter 20
Coyote's Life is a Beach

After the convention, Coyote and Coyote Woman took a weekend vacation to a quiet little spring Coyote knew about on the western slope of the Cascades. He relaxed by the campfire and listened to the water bubbling out of the ground and watched the sparks fly upward toward the invisible plume of sulfur off the mountain's cone. Coyote Woman sat with her back against a western red cedar opening a stack of contribution envelopes and recording the amounts on her powerful laptop PC. Then she lay back on her sleeping bag and put her hands behind her head. "That was a great convention, Coyote," she said.

Coyote smiled and reached over toward her. As he did so he knocked a stack of checks off a rock and they floated toward the fire.

Coyote reached out and deflected them, singeing the back of his paw. The checks fluttered down around him.

One check settled in the fur front of his nose. It was drawn on the account of MC Enterprises, Inc.

Coyote's hair lay down all over his back, and an old weakness crept into his knees, like he was standing in warm soup.

Could MC be the same Mavis Clovis he had pursued so ardently in her Small-Town Teenager years, telling her story after story to enthrall her? The same Mavis Clovis that he had seen fervently writing a story that he had never seen published, though he had read every literary magazine in North America? The same Mavis Clovis to whom he had given a taxicab ride from New York City to Cuzco, Peru? The same Mavis Clovis who recited poetry by heart? The same Mavis Clovis he had dreamed about before and since, but couldn't find?

"Say, what is this MC Enterprises?" Coyote asked, feigning nonchalance.

"Strange you should ask," Coyote Woman said. "They are one of your biggest contributors. They are a huge pharmaceutical company, I hear. Privately held."

Coyote lay on his back and, as the water tumbled and the sparks flew, he felt as if he were now lying in a vat of warm soup. He tucked the check into his fur and watched the sparks fly upward, past the crowns of the impossibly tall western red cedars, past the smoldering fingers of the

Cascades, all the way up to the perfectly clear anthracite sky, to merge with the diamonds of the stars.

The next morning Coyote was gone.

The Florida corporate complex of MC Enterprises, Inc. was surprisingly modest—thirty acres of solar-powered offices, laboratories, manufacturing, and warehouse space covered in mirrored sun-reflecting thermopane nestled into a grove of cabbage palms on the edge of the Everglades—considering that the D&B report had indicated sales of over 5 billion dollars. The modest three-panel brochure in the lobby told the company story. It featured a colorful sketch of a woman standing in a jungle with fern fronds tastefully arrayed in front of her, discussing her first products with the jungle people of Peru. The last panel showed a photograph of the board of directors: thirteen tribal leaders and the same woman, dressed in Brooks Brothers for Women. Although she was in the background in both cases, it was clear to Coyote who she was. She was not skinny. She was round and full. It was Mavis Clovis, the woman of his dreams.

Coyote asked the receptionist if Ms. Clovis was in.

"Aren't you Coyote, the candidate?" exclaimed the woman wearing a tastefully miniature phone headset.

"No," said Coyote.

"You are too," she said. "President Clovis is not available. She is on leave of absence until further notice. You know, this business practically runs itself anyway. She can do what she wants."

"Where is she?"

"She's in the Virgin Islands somewhere, studying sea urchins or coral or some such slimy thing. Climate's changing you know. She doesn't want to be disturbed."

Coyote was gone.

Coyote scuba-dived into a secluded bay on the north side of a Virgin Island.

"Say, buddy," Coyote bubbled to a six-foot barracuda idling in front of him still as a Bowie knife in a store display. "Yeah," said the barracuda, "she's here. On the beach. Good luck. I've been trying to get her attention for weeks. Nothing."

Coyote was cruising along the lower reaches of the reef, at thirty feet. Excited by barracuda's news, he turned toward the surface, got too close to the reef and banged his knees on some fire coral, "Aaiee!," he bubbled, and stroked toward shore, rising slowly until the white sands ran up underneath him and he could feel the gentle rolling of the swells.

He saw the grains of soft white sand tumble back and forth, back and forth, tumbling silently until they disappeared into the rhythm of the sea.

He poked his head through the surface of the water and stood up. He dropped his regulator from his mouth. He pulled off his mask. He looked around.

The white sand beach was totally secluded, surrounded on three sides by thick green leafy hills steaming in the August heat. The fourth side was a white sand beach protected by the reef. There were no boats in the bay. There were no houses in the woods. There were no people on the beach.

Except one.

Propped up with her back against a little mound of sand, reading a book, was Mavis Clovis.

Her arms and legs glistened with oil in the sun. Her hair, still wet from her last dive, streamed away from her head toward a pile of scuba gear on the beach. Her book was thick and scholarly, and as she slowly turned a page Coyote noticed a cool breeze ruffle his wet fur. As he stepped higher onto the sand, he also noticed that, except for a funky pair of shades, Mavis Clovis was naked as the day she was born.

Coyote fell over. The sudden weakening of his knees had compounded other developing problems. The first was the fire coral stings on his knees. They burned like local forest fires. Worse was the weight. Once out of water, Coyote was heavy as a freight train. Bad enough he was wearing dual steel air tanks on his back, but his natural buoyancy had required him to wear a megaton of lead weights to keep him under water. (Now you know why more Coyotes don't scuba-dive). He looked like Pancho Villa festooned with straps of lead weights.

When he fell over, he was down for good, like a turtle on its back.

"Aieee," he groaned. He couldn't reach the damn weight releases. Clearly he had never been officially scuba certified or this wouldn't have happened. He wanted to call out to her but for two problems. First, even he had the inkling that his dignity was somewhat compromised at the moment—not the dramatic reentry into her life he had in mind. Second, she was still far down the beach and she probably couldn't hear his howls anyway.

He struggled to extricate himself, straining to get the weights and tanks unhooked from his body, until, exhausted by the flailing and the swimming and the hot sun and the soft sound of seawater lapping at the beach, he fell asleep.

He dreamed.

He dreamed that he slowly stirred awake, his eyes out of focus. He dreamed that as his vision cleared, he saw that he was in a tent. The tent had a wooden floor and canvas roof but otherwise was open on all four sides, covered by a fine gauze of mosquito netting. Outside dripped lush foliage, green piled upon green, accented with bursts of paradise flowers and hibiscus. The air was redolent with incense. The late afternoon sun filtered through the trees.

The tent was cool. One side contained two freestanding bookshelves crammed with texts, microscopes, slide trays, and other apparatus. Opposite, a desk held a lamp and a Macintosh laptop. Otherwise, there was only a bed in the center. He dreamed that he was in it.

Next to him, curled up snug and tight against him, her arm and her leg draped over him, her light rhythmic breathing punctuated by an occasional slight snore, was Mavis Clovis.

He woke up. And this time it was true.

He clutched her, hard, while a vibration identical with the tuning fork of the universe swept through him. Her eyes opened. "Hi," she said.

"Before you say anything, I have something to tell you," she said, a little sheepishly. "I'd like you to meet my boyfriend, Teddy."

Coyote's fur stood straight up as he heard a voice behind him. "Hello, Coyote," it said.

He wheeled around. There in a cage in the corner was a small green parrot with an iridescent red patch on his forehead. As Coyote stared at him, he thought that the patch glowed with a little extra heat.

"Teddy's my friend," Mavis said. "I've told him all your stories." She quickly hopped out of bed and placed a towel over the cage. "Good night, Teddy," she said.

She stood over Coyote, lying heavy as an ocean on the bed, and smiled somewhat sheepishly. Her bronze skin glistened, her breasts dripped with nurturing perspiration, her thighs revealed a glistening jungle trail, pulsing and radiantly alive.

He could neither breathe nor move, yet rose to her, at once mad, leaden and on fire.

Their eyes could not tolerate all they saw there before their skins could not comprehend all they felt there. Their eyes pulled closed by the weight of impossible sensations. Their growls rose to matching pitched howls that shook crabs from the mangroves, set the fecund world on fire and drained the sum of evolution toward joy.

Coyote stayed with her forever, although time was a tumble.

She was finishing her dissertation on the population dynamics of spiny sea urchins, trying to prove her hypothesis that their population decline was an indicator of poor reef health from the heating effects of climate change.

Every morning they would dive on the reef and observe the creatures as they appeared to reduce and enlarge their physical size relative to their population pressures. Mavis would record her detailed observations and measurements on her plastic underwater slate. Then she and Coyote would steal off to frolic among the groupers and morays and angelfish.

Each evening Coyote would tell her stories while Mavis compiled her data for her dissertation onto her Macintosh.

Each night Coyote would tumble into a vat of warm sour cream, into a vat of molten gold, into a vat of astonished jellyfish, into a deep black well of ecstatic weariness that reached into the shadows of his marrow, into the space of his birth.

One night they decided to go for a night dive. They entered the water with electric torches and sucked and exhaled like spacemen as they disappeared under the silver surface of the moonlight. Along the reef, they cupped their hands over sleeping fish, scratched the whiskers of lobsters and let sleeping turtles lie.

Mavis then signaled Coyote to turn off their torches. For a moment they completely disappeared. Coyote lay in the neutral black space of the saltwater and knew that he had a deep ancestral memory of this feeling. And then another ancestral memory appeared before him. He saw Mavis Clovis.

Or he didn't see Mavis Clovis, but rather her swirling absence. She was dancing in the water, moving her arms and legs like a Balinese enchantress, then whirling her whole body around like a dervish. How did he know?

Her movements excited tiny bioluminescent organisms in the water, which lit up her paint swirls of water. Coyote watched, dumfounded, as Mavis danced and whirled and exploded, she and the cool silent bio life limning the creation of the universe while their silver air bubbles together tracked the earth's gravity upward to the surface, then spilled over onto the cool image of the moon.

So this what demon lovers do, thought Coyote.

Chapter 21
Rain on Coyote's Parade

Mavis touched up the concluding paragraph on the Mac. Her thesis was done. Time to go.

She and Coyote and Teddy packed their gear into duffels, closed the camp, and flew to St. Thomas. Then from the Virgin Islands to Puerto Rico. There they boarded a plane for Miami. Coyote and Mavis held hands the entire plane ride, looking out the window, oblivious to the chatter in Spanish around them.

At the arrival terminal, an enormous celebration was going on. Mavis walked into the arrival lounge with Teddy on her shoulder. As Coyote stepped in after her, duffel of scuba gear over his shoulder, there was a huge cheer and electronic flashes went off around him like exploding stars.

"What?" blinked Coyote.

His eyes cleared. Men and women talked rapidly into microphones. Shoulder-held TV cameras danced in his face. A huge mob surrounded the gate, held back by a cordon of uniformed policemen. And Coyote Woman rushed up to greet him.

"Smile, Coyote," she whispered into his ear as she kissed his cheek. "We won."

"What?" said Coyote. He swung down the duffel. Suddenly it weighed a ton. His arm was killing him.

Then he stood up fast. Up ahead with the other passengers filing toward the main terminal walked Mavis Clovis, tan as a jungle palm, fragrant as gardenias, beautiful as hibiscus and bougainvillea, jungle bio-pharmacologist extraordinaire, friend of jungle tribes, the reigning expert on the spiny sea urchin, the teller of stories to parrots. And woman of his dreams.

Oblivious to Coyote's predicament, she turned the corner with the other passengers, hurried past the cameras and the crowd, and disappeared into thin air.

It rained on Coyote's victory parade. But the public didn't mind.

Coyote drove slowly in the Thunderbird, smiling and waving. But he felt like the coyote he once saw at the zoo. The real thing, to be sure, but really not. It was curled up in a soft furry ball, its tail wrapped around its body and over its eyes, sleeping. Sleeping until the immediate nightmare of the bars of the cage and the cotton candy hoards would go away. Sleeping so he could dream of pouncing over the tumbleweed, hiding behind the sagebrush, stealing yapping poodles off suburban back porches, and pursuing the woman of his dreams.

Truth is, Coyote served the nation well. For nearly four years he regaled the populace with stories and odd behavior. He never compromised freedom. And otherwise didn't do much damage. The people loved him. Baby Coyote was a hit. And the grinning assassin's bullet didn't really hurt at all.

Epilogue
Coyote Tells a Story

Mavis Clovis was in her studio painting. This painting wasn't bad, she thought, although the twenty grand or so her dealer would get for it seemed excessive.

But if people were willing to pay for the images that came to her, that was not her affair. She painted what she pleased. She sometimes wondered if people might want to read her stories too, now stored on her computer. Screw it, she was keeping those to herself for now.

While she painted, her assistant, Teddy the parrot, perused the catalogue of her latest exhibition. "I like the last picture the best," he squawked.

"Which one is that?" she asked.

"The one that shows a coyote sleeping in a sort of beach setting, surrounded by cedars and pines and trout and flickers, but the beach is also a bed on which lies a sleeping nude under a sunset of sinuous blue mountains. And in the ferns there's this incredibly handsome parrot observing the scene."

"That one's not too bad," she said.

"At least it ain't no damn abstraction," Teddy said.

Mavis had been surprised at the success of her paintings, really only a hobby she took up to fill the empty hours after finishing her Ph.D. and selling her fifty percent of MC Enterprises to her fellow board members for mega millions cash. She had invested the proceeds in habitat conservation through the Nature Conservancy and the Audubon society and the Native American Rights Fund while endowing chairs in ethnopharmacology and humor research at several universities throughout the Americas. Those studies should be fun, she thought. Then she dropped out of sight.

But she couldn't escape notoriety. When it struck, the dynamic of the art market immediately jacked up the price of her paintings. One week her paintings, which a small entrepreneurial gallery had taken on exclusive contract and marked at $500, were the next marked at $5000. And going up. Here's how it happened.

Months after Coyote was shot a reporter turned up on her doorstep tracking down the rumor that President Coyote had had a jungle lover. These rumors had persisted throughout the Coyote administration. Headlines had periodically scorched *The National Enquirer*, *The Star*, *The Weekly World News,* and *People,* while very lengthy analytic pieces appeared in *The Atlantic* and the *Lakota Times.* Until now, no one could confirm the identity of the mystery woman.

She had been happy laying low. Coyote was a public figure, and she didn't want to screw up his agenda, whatever it was. She was quite content in her apartment, painting and writing. But she knew the journalistic sharks were circling. Finally, one of them attacked.

She refused the interview, of course, but the salivating reporter did get in one question. "Ms. Clovis, Ms. Clovis, please. If you claim you've never met Coyote, how is it that he is always in your paintings?" Clearly, he was proud of himself. He had done his homework. On a tip, he had visited the small, unknown gallery. What he saw there had set his pen and notebook on fire.

"Imagination," she answered, and slammed the door.

Nevertheless, the national press frenzy sent her painting prices spiraling.

The journalistic sharks managed to find her but neither they nor the police ever did get a bite out of Coyote's attempted assassin. He was described by eyewitnesses as tall and erect, with an obnoxious laugh. But he proved simply too fast to catch. Whoever he was, he had done Coyote a favor.

Coyote checked out of office at a good time. His popularity was still high. The Party Brass was clamoring for him to run again. But after nearly four years in office, though his antic good humor was continuing to entertain, amuse, and mystify the populace, the press was beginning to seriously hone in on his accomplishments, which looked embarrassingly thin. "Is the role of a President only to keep the country laughing?" questioned the editorialists. "What about Stopping Communism, or Stopping Terrorism, or Stopping Inflation, or Stopping Stagflation, or Stopping Unemployment, or Stopping Regulation, or Stopping Deregulation, or Stopping False Advertising for Drainpipe Cleaner?" "Hey," responded Coyote in his weekly one AM radio conversation with America, "let me tell you a story."

Some pundits were now referring to the Coyote Era as a sideshow. His nocturnal habits disturbed a significant number of the power elite, all early risers. Coyote knew he was not particularly effective during the day. He'd show up at the odd Senate hearing or National Press Club luncheon or Rose Garden ceremony, but nobody gave him high marks. But he'd perform adequately in local, regional, and national ribbon cuttings, where he'd cut quite a figure in his red, white, and blue tuxedo coat left over from his circus days, his beaded bill cap, his high-topped sneakers, and his shades, driving his Thunderbird. And the nation loved Baby Coyote, the subject of a picture story in *People* at least once a month.

It was the PRESIDENT'S ALL NIGHT TALK RADIO SHOW that had the mainstream press depressed.

"What is with this guy?" questioned the *Washington Times*. "Our reporters are exhausted staying up late listening every night. And then all he does is listen to other people's stories and tell his own. Off color ones, at that."

"Colorful ones, at that," said the *Washington Post.*

Mavis listened in her bed every night, but resisted the persistent urge to call in with a story or poem of her own. She knew President Coyote would be a goner if she did.

She heard the last wandering story Coyote told before he left the air for good. It was long and rambling, but one of his best, she thought. At least it had some kind of an ending. She curled up and remembered.

Coyote was going along, hungry as a Coyote, his stomach rumbling like thunder. "Hey, nice day," he said to the grasses. "Nice day," he said to the rocks. "Nice day," he said to the river he was passing by.

"No, it's not," said Mouse from the deep grass of the riverbank.

"Why not?" said Coyote, stopped short, listening, licking his lips.

"Because I want to cross the river and I can't," replied the mouse voice, annoyed.

"Why do you want to cross the river?"

"Because I need to get to the other side, asshole. What's wrong with you, Coyote?"

"OK, OK, relax," said Coyote, recognizing the voice of Annoying Mouse, a bitter one. "What's happening on the other side?"

"Well, see, I went to my dermatologist 'cause I had this bad itch, see, always just out of reach, see, and it was driving

me crazy. So he gives me a series of gunks which fail miserably. So he sends me to an acupuncturist. He puts me so full of holes I feel like a pincushion. All I get is needle nightmares."

"Why not get a back scratcher?"

"Very funny, Whiskerbreath. Of course that's the first thing I tried. Didn't stop it. So he sends me to the rapist. I'm sorry, a 'therapist.' A Jungian, it turns out, whatever that is. She tells me no problem, just go into The Hills and Get High. A vacation I don't need, says I, and if you are thinking I'll do drugs?!? I didn't say a vacation or drugs, says she. Just climb up into The Black Hills and look around, see what you see. So finally I says OK, 'cause I figure anything's gotta be cheaper than shrink bills. But now I can't get past this river. Is that clear enough for you, Bushleaguetail?"

Coyote looked over the river to the horizon. Indeed, there did loom an anomalous agglomeration of dark green and granite peaks rising out of the dusty flatness. "Are those The Hills?" Coyote asked.

"Do you see any other ones, Furface?" Mouse responded chippily.

"Look," said Coyote, "if you don't knock off the scummy comments, I'll gulp you down now and be done with it."

"You look, Coyote. I'm not asking for favors. Maybe I'm procrastinating. Maybe I don't really want to look around. Maybe I like being miserable. Huh? Huh? And maybe I don't care what you do. So just leave me alone and get back on your lazy way. OK?"

"Boy, you could really piss a guy off," Coyote said. "I could eat you right now. Munching mice is one of my Great Things. But I have to admit, I'm not going to eat you. You're way too bitter. I'd get indigestion."

"Thanks a lot, Drooptongue."

"I don't need this abuse," Coyote said, trotting off, "but talk to that turtle over there. He may help you across. I'll be seeing you."

"Not if I see you first, Bushbreath! What turtle over where?" Mouse looked around, then looked back. Coyote was gone.

Lazing in the slow-moving margins of the river was a large painted turtle. His back was a blue-green circle, his belly a riot of neon. His head was a turtle head, except that it may have had some small whiskers on either side of its nose.

He offered to ferry Mouse across the river.

"That's OK," said Mouse, "I have some other things to do."

"OK," said Turtle, "but I'm pulling out."

At the last moment, Mouse hopped on his back. Turtle moved out into the river.

Mouse was terrified. "Uh, Turtle, you are aware, I hope, that I can't swim. Swimming is not part of my Original Equipment Package."

"Mouse," said Turtle, "you are aware, I believe, that carrying around an asshole is not part of my Original Equipment Package."

"OK, OK, just checking," said Mouse, looking around him at the tiny whitecaps lapping the reeds.

"But," said Turtle, "I am a businessman. There is a fee for this crossing."

"A fee? A fee! Now you tell me. A fee? How am I going to come up with a fee? I don't have anything on me. Not a dime. Not a sou. Not a seed. Nothing. Nothing at all. OK, OK, take me back."

"You have to give me something, smart guy."

"What do I have? Nothing. Didn't you hear me? I'm broke."

"How about a pound of flesh?" smiled Turtle.

"Very funny, Shylock. But I only weigh an ounce and a half. I know, I weighed myself yesterday. I watch my weight carefully. No kidding. That's it. An ounce and a half. That's forty-two in grams."

"You must give me something," said Turtle. "Getting where you want to go ain't free. Do you have a tale?"

"A tail. Of course I have a tail. But I'm attached to it. I like it. Looks real good under a suit. It's not for sale."

"Cool it," said Turtle, idling in the current of the river. Mouse felt the whitecaps splashing higher on the shell. "Tell me a story."

"Oh, a tale? A tale! Ha, ha, a tale! Sure, OK, a story. HMMM. Wait a minute, I don't know any stories. I mean, not good ones. I'm one of those kinds of guys that forgets jokes even. You know the type. Everyone's telling dirty jokes at the party,

and you laugh and laugh. The next day, gone. I should write them down. Really, I should write them down."

Turtle dumped him into the water.

For someone who couldn't swim, Mouse was well motivated to learn. Fortunately, he was actually quite close to the opposite bank, and scrambled through the reeds to the sandy shore, wet for the first time in his life, and exhausted, not for the first time.

He cursed Turtle two or three times while he shook his fur and dried off in the sun. Then he noticed that he felt pretty good. He looked at the river, its silver surface curling by among the stalks of reeds. He never felt better. In fact, he felt like jumping in again. But he didn't.

Instead he headed out toward the Black Hills shimmering through the heatwaves in the distance.

He ran as fast as he could. Really hustled. Figured he had it made now. This would be easier than he thought. But it wasn't. He ran into a giant freeway barrier, Interstate 90.

Parallel ribbons of concrete undulated to the horizons. Huge Pacific Intermountain Express tanker trucks hurtled over them hauling glacial water to Los Angeles to sell by the glassful. Overheating family sedans pulled palatial camper trailers with bicycles strapped on the top and kids lying inside watching TV and puking. Family cars with no trailers raced by them all, stuffed to the ceiling with fighting children and exasperated parents attempting to interest them in their surroundings by prodding with the eternal question, "Which Granite Head on Mount Rushmore do you want to see most?" while the kids played pocket video games and refused to share CDs for their Discmen.

Mouse didn't stand a chance. He settled under a forlorn roadside tree planted by Lady Bird Johnson and assessed the situation.

He reached into his pocket. Only a few bucks cash, plus credit cards. Hey, he wasn't going to tell that Turtle everything. His Delta Airlines Frequent Flyer card fell out on the ground. Can't use that now, he said. Left over from his dyspeptic salesman days when he regularly earned free tickets. He scored so many he sold them on the black market in the Wall Street Journal. But out here even his Visa, MasterCard, and American Express cards were useless. And he was getting hungry.

He wandered parallel to the interstate looking for an opening until his feet screamed at him and he was nearly dead from the heat. He was about to give up and turn back when he saw a gas station up ahead.

The pump area was full of enormous idling diesels and trailers. He avoided them and sneaked into the garage area to look for a drink. He hopped up on the drinking fountain and had a nice chilled squirt. When he hopped down he noticed someone underneath the body of a rusted out Chevy.

"Damn," mumbled the voice under the car, "this beast is sick. I'm convinced it's the timing. Timing is the key. I used to not think about it. Just had it. Worked in comedy clubs all over the country. I'd be deadpanning, they'd be falling off their

chairs. And now my car breaks down. Again. Not funny. I've lost it."

"Yeah," said Mouse, "I've heard the comedy business really sucks. Hand to mouth, hand to mouth."

Buffalo eased out from under the car on a little four-wheeled truck.

"Say, Little One, I didn't say it sucked. I just said I've lost my timing."

"OK, OK," said Mouse. "Don't be so touchy. If life is so good, why you driving this scummy beater?"

"Are you kidding me? This car is a beauty. A Reagan-era double-overhead scamshaft Buy American plus trickle-down roomy economics buggy. This Chevy had two hundred fifty bucks written on the windshield. Lots of rust. Runs good. Only the last part was a lie. If I can fix the timing, why throw it away?"

"What are you doing here?" asked Mouse.

"I'm on my way to a gig in Keystone. In the Black Hills. Opening act for a rock and roll concert at the Black Hills outdoor amphitheater. Rose and the Res Girls. Heard of 'em? They're hot. Big break for me. So of course my car breaks down. I neglected to bring adequate cash so the mechanic is letting me fool with it myself. But I don't know which way a horsepower whinnies."

"Timing? If that's your only problem, I know all that stuff," said Mouse. "Christ, I didn't grow up around farmers for nothing. Those guys can fix anything. So can I."

Mouse crawled under the hood. He quickly located the timing chain. He called for tools, which Buffalo passed to him.

An hour later they were on the road. Buffalo was wedged behind the wheel. Mouse would have had plenty of room on the seat next to him but for the fat bags of Doritos, Fritos, and potato chips there plus a large can of honey-roasted peanuts and three or four Cokes. Buffalo was a big guy. Mouse ate his fill of that crap in about a second.

Mouse eventually sat on a cellophane bag and watched Buffalo drive along quietly, although the speedometer was reading 90 miles per hour. Buffalo glanced over and smiled, at which point Mouse noticed, and then forgot, his unusually long whiskers.

"I suppose you do a lot of fat jokes," said Mouse, feeling conversational. "The self-deprecating stuff. How about the put down? That's hot. And sex jokes? Sex jokes always get 'em. Love 'em myself."

"Fat jokes? Naah. Why would I do that? And I don't insult the audience either. What for? Not much sex either. I'm generally not interested. Except in the fall. Then I gotta admit it's all I can think about. It gets so bad then I gotta knock off the comedy circuit entirely for a couple weeks and go out and butt heads and chase tail. Talk about a rut."

Oh, oh, thought Mouse. A punster. Booooring.

"No, I just tell stories. I've always been the funny guy. Born entertainer. The fat kid in school with the belly laugh. But now it's becoming like work. I mean, nothing is striking me as

funny," he said as he inhaled another bag of Fritos. "I'm not even too enthusiastic about this upcoming gig. I've been dying out there."

They drove on, both quiet as mice, brooding as buffalo.

The dry, cracked moonscape of the Badlands slowly gave way to cool Black Hills rising up around them. They were surrounded by green lush towers of granite and dense forests of black evergreens. Buffalo rolled to a stop on the main street of Keystone, South Dakota.

"Keystone," he announced. "Either it's a tacky tourist town or the key to the continent, who knows. Of course names aren't everything. Right nearby are towns named Deadwood and Spearfish. Hey, could I make that up? Lots of people go to see those four granite heads near Deadwood, if you get my drift. But I visit that Spearfish shrine every time I'm here," he said, reaching for another bag of chips.

"Get me out of here," Mouse laughed. Buffalo pulled over.

"Thanks for the lift. I was dying out there. So to speak. Heh, heh. Get it?" Buffalo looked at him deadpan. "Yeah," he said. "Timing is everything."

"Say, what time's your gig today?" asked Mouse, warming up. "Maybe I could be there."

"You don't seem like a comedy kind of guy," said Buffalo.

"Well, a depressed chip-snorting buffalo isn't my first idea of a big laugh, either. I'm sorta curious."

"OK," said Buffalo. "Sunset. At the new Keystone Amphitheater. It's around here somewhere. MC Productions is

big time. I hear it's sold out, but I suspect a gentleman of your stature can sneak in. I can use a sympathetic audience. But I probably won't notice you, no offense."

"If I'm there, you'll know it," said Mouse. He slammed the door and waved. Buffalo smiled and farted as he and the Chevy purred up the street. They were running like a charm.

Mouse struck out along the first road leading up toward the top of the Hills. He hiked along a deeply shadowed drainage ditch as it rose toward the slit of bright blue sky overhead. He passed by campgrounds spanning creeks and huge open meadows with buffalo grazing in the distance. He passed log cabins next to dammed trout ponds where you could fish rainbow trout for a $5 fee. He passed a rainbow billboard for Mountain Hydro. He came to a curio shop surrounded by concrete teepees and totem poles and headdresses. Signs promised that inside was a complete selection of handcrafted Indian and Western curios and shells from oceans around the world. "See the man-eating giant clam! Meet Buffalo Bill! See Black Elk tell a story!"

"See Black Elk tell a story? Don't they mean hear him?" thought Mouse.

Mouse entered, strolling under the saloon-type doors. Before he knew it, he had purchased a little plastic box of Mexican jumping beans, a necklace of sea urchin spines, and a comic book of Black Hills mythology. That plus a Snickers bar sucked his wallet absolutely dry of cash. He hadn't noticed until too late that no credit cards were accepted.

He wandered around further, among racks of wooden toy guns and feather headdresses handmade in Taiwan. In the back of the store two men sat across from each other playing cards. They looked like Cézanne's painting, "The Card Players." Except one was Buffalo Bill and the other was Black Elk.

Mouse strolled up. Bill had just been ginned by Black Elk. He was fuming. Black Elk had perspective. "Cards is cards," he said.

Mouse sat in on the next hand while he inquired about how to get where he was going.

"To the top of the tallest Peak?" said Buffalo Bill. "What for? If I were you, I'd turn around and catch Rose and the Res Girls at the Outdoor. They're hot. Nothing up on that peak but wind and rain."

Black Elk looked at Mouse. "You got a gin," he said. Mouse was startled and looked at his cards. Damned if he didn't. Buffalo Bill cursed again and pulled a pint of jalapeño lemonade from underneath his chair. The buckskin fringes on his jacket swished back and forth as he drank.

Black Elk escorted Mouse to the parking lot in front. As he appeared through the door children bolted out of campers and overstuffed cars and crowded around him. "Are you a real Indian?" they asked.

"Hang on a secint, kids, and I'll tell you all about it."

He pointed Mouse in a direction directly up the side of the mountain following a powerline trail. "Much faster," he said.

"Don't these stupid kids piss you off?" Mouse asked. "What stupid kids?" Black Elk answered, and returned to the children. He sat down among them and spun them stories of Iktome the Trickster spider and of White Buffalo Calf Woman and the gift of the sacred pipe. During the stories, not one smartass kid said a word. The parents, napping blissfully in their idling camper vans, paid up handsomely at the end.

Mouse climbed up the trail beneath the humming and crackling power line. Power line pylons marched like angle-iron robots over the hills as far as he could see in either direction. It was tough going. The ground was rocky and full of lairs for snakes. Finally he reached the top of a saddleback and watched the pylons march off to the western horizon and the faint irregular outline of the Rocky Mountains and the dim murmur of the Pacific surf beyond. Behind him they fanned out to the eastern horizon of Badlands and wheat fields and enormous forests and tall cities in the distance. Another army of power pylons marched away from him to the south, skirting Denver and ski areas and sand dunes and deserts and canyons. To the north they swept through swamps and flax fields and lakes and tundra and permafrost and glaciers.

As Mouse continued to climb and admire the view around him, he suddenly had a premonition that he was being watched. The fur rose up on the back of his neck. As he slowly looked over his shoulder, he saw something terrifying.

Four huge stone heads were staring at him over the treetops. They looked right at him out of their huge hollow irises. Roosevelt. Jefferson. Washington. Lincoln. "Jesus," Mouse whistled. He felt his fur lay down on his little back in awe and admiration. He hiked up the side of the saddleback to get a better look.

The trail first led back into deep forest—huge pines and spruces and hemlocks blocked out the sun—and then emerged into a higher meadow. The stone heads should have been just over the rise.

But instead he saw in the distance straight ahead of him another stone mountain. It too was carved. It too told a story. It was Crazy Horse. He was astride a horse that rode out of the base of a mountain. His arm was thrust forward. His head was tossed back in a cry of agony and pain.

Mouse climbed further. He came to the shore of a deep black lake surrounded by dense forest. He was so hot from climbing. He stood on the shore on a large boulder. He looked down from it into the crystal-clear water where he could see the boulder-strewn bottom thirty feet below. And the fish. Schools of cutthroat trout angled between the dark rocks. "They may want to eat me," thought Mouse. "Particularly that big one," he thought about a giant Rainbow floating by. Possibly it winked.

But he remembered the feeling he had after the swim in the stream. He had felt renewed, as if he had put on a whole new skin. The lake water shimmered and shone and beckoned before him in the sun. And there was no one around. He stripped off his clothes and dove in. It was ice cold.

He felt his heart seize. He felt his ankles and wrists and neck begin to ache. He felt his body growing numb. And he felt ecstatic.

He burst through the surface and raced back onto the boulder. He stood there shivering, looking into the ripples of his wake. The school of cutthroats looked back at him and rolled away. The giant Rainbow arced out of the water in the distance and smiled. The warm sun penetrated his fur, and he slowly felt as if he were rising off this rock, dissolving into the water and the air.

He dove in again. And again. Then he slept on the warm rock.

Late in the day he climbed further, continuing up the saddleback as the trees fell away. As he emerged from the last stand of gnarled pines, a flicker laughed and dropped a feather as it flew out in front of him. Mouse picked it up. Its red shaft was the color of sunset. He tucked it behind his ear.

The trail was strewn with boulders. Growth was reduced to small shrubs clinging to rocks. Then nothing at all. Only bare rock. Smooth granite rock. And the wind blew cold and strong. He shivered. He had left his clothes back at the lake. He clung to the granite and climbed straight up.

He paused on a rock ledge and looked around. He saw again the power lines fanning out to the four directions, this time like a great spiderweb with its center the dark mountains below him. He saw the parts in the hair of Roosevelt, Jefferson, Washington, Lincoln. He looked into the hollow mouth and the stricken eyes of Crazy Horse.

Then he noticed that the ledge he was standing on was not a natural ledge. It too had been carved. He looked up. He spied the fringes of a huge furry granite presence above him. "Well, well," he said, "Fancy meeting you here." And he climbed.

He climbed right into the stone mouth of Coyote. He looked out. He had the highest perspective in the heart of the continent.

The sun winked. A rainbow smiled beneath the skirts of a rain cloud. Puffy clouds strolled up to say hello.

And as he looked around further, he noticed the subtle curves of Mother Earth. She caressed the horizon. She was the turtle's back. A laughing babe. A furball, soft as home.

He finally got it. The Big Joke. And it was a good one. All this time he was worrying Mother Earth was having a ball.

He threw his head back and began to laugh. He howled his arrival. He howled his joy.

As he howled, he heard answering laughter well up from the valley far below. It was Buffalo, warming up the crowd for Rose and the Res Girls at the Keystone Amphitheater. From here, he could see the sold-out crowd. Turtle, Trout Mother, Flicker, and Thunderbird were all there. They were rolling in the aisles.

Mavis awoke at first light. She dressed with the memory of the story fresh in her mind. She grabbed some orange juice and a piece of toast for her and lobbed a McIntosh apple to Teddy. She began to paint.

At noon she put down her brushes. She always quit at noon while she was still on fire. That way her creative juices flowed through the next day and the next. And she was hungry as a fox.

She wandered over to her loft window and stood next to Teddy looking out over the park. It stretched out in front of them, on and on, encompassing prairies and mountains and lakes and meadows and boulders and clouds, touching both oceans. In it kids were playing and workers working and mimes miming and muggers mugging and dancers dancing.

She returned to the easel. This was her 20th painting in the Coyote Series. She wondered what number 21 would be.

She fed Teddy a brown banana from the bowl next to the refrigerator. That's all there was. Damn. She would have to go out shopping. She hated shopping.

She thought about Coyote. About how he hustled her like a crazy man when she was a high school drama star, how he told her stories she never forgot, how his enflamed curiosity often touched the molten core of a good idea. About his antic irresponsibility. About his nice touch. And about how somehow, he kept coming back, time and time again, with that persistent laugh. He made a fine President, she smiled to herself, but a horseshit researcher.

She suddenly heard a strange roaring wind outside. She ran back to the window and watched its whirling advance. A tornado? In Central Park? No way.

But on it came.

It was heading right for her building and she was just beginning to react, to slam windows, shut doors, turn on the emergency radio, find the flashlight, take cover, when it stopped, and there was a flash of red parked at the curb. She recognized it immediately. A '56 Thunderbird.

At the same moment there was a knock at her door. She crossed the room and opened it. It was her dealer. "Is the next painting done yet?" asked Coyote Woman as she strode in. "I think I have a buyer for the whole series."

Outside the window, a howling rose up from the vicinity of the curbed tornado. It was a howling that sounded like laughter.

THE END

2026 Author's Note

These tales were first written down over forty years ago, as several anachronisms will attest— answering machines, Polaroid photographs, black landline telephone, flashbulbs, etc. And I failed to mention above two additional important influences. Protean linguist Jaime de Angulo lived with several California indigenous communities and mastered not only their languages but some of the oral tradition, which he recited in 1949 over KPFA radio, later published as *Indian Tales*, a beloved book recommended to me by Gary Snyder in 1969 which I read multiple times to all our children, the animal people and oral rhythms enchanting us all. The second is *Seven Arrows* (1972), by Hyemeyohsts Storm from which my psyche freely adapted his story of Jumping Mouse for this collection.

After close calls at two major publishers, *Coyote and the Thunderbird* disappeared into the drawer of forgotten things as a fourth child filled out the family as did a responsible job on the *Star Tribune* editorial board. Retired now and having published many collections of poems, poetry anthologies, and personal essays chosen from my newspaper column *The Urban Coyote,* I am deeply grateful to publisher Ian Leask of Calumet Editions for relentlessly badgering me to bring these stories out of retirement and into the light. As I rediscovered upon rereading them, they are indeed literally timeless, psychic energy pursuing its tail and creating the world. Gratitude also to Calumet Editions tech genius Josh Weber for rescuing several files locked up tight in an ancient version of MS Word, freeing them to howl here.

About the Author

After a career in academia, marketing communications, and journalism on the editorial board of the *Star Tribune*, where he won several Page One awards for excellence, since 2000 Lenfestey has published eight collections of poems, two collections of personal essays, edited three poetry anthologies, and co-edited *Robert Bly in This World* (University of Minnesota Press). His play with Jon Cranney, "Coyote Discovers America," opened the 25th season of the Minneapolis Children's Theater Company. His *haibun* memoir, *Seeking the Cave: A Pilgrimage to Cold Mountain* (Milkweed Editions) was a finalist for the 2014 Minnesota Book Award. His sixth poetry collection, *A Marriage Book: 50 Years of Poems from a Marriage* (Milkweed Editions), was a finalist for two 2017 Midwest book awards. In 2020 he received the Kay Sexton Award for significant contributions and leadership in the Minnesota Literary Community. In November 2024 Milkweed Editions published his eighth poetry collection, *Time Remaining: Body Odes, Praise Songs, Oddities, Amazements.* For fifteen years he chaired the popular Literary Witnesses poetry program Minneapolis and led a summer poetry series on Mackinac Island, Michigan. He currently serves on the boards of Red Dragonfly Press in Minnesota, the Hellbender Poetry Gathering in North Carolina, and is the founder of Poets, Writers, Musicians Against the War on the Earth. He lives in Minneapolis with his wife, the journalist Susan Lenfestey. They have four children and ten grandchildren.

www.coyotepoet.com

www.ingramcontent.com/pod-product-compliance
Lightning Source LLC
LaVergne TN
LVHW091051080826
845145LV00002B/710

* 9 7 8 1 9 6 2 8 3 4 7 1 1 *